PENGUIN CLASSICS

Maigret's Childhood Friend

'I love reading Simenon. He makes me think of Chekhov'
– William Faulkner

'A truly wonderful writer . . . marvellously readable – lucid, simple, absolutely in tune with the world he creates'
– Muriel Spark

'Few writers have ever conveyed with such a sure touch, the bleakness of human life'
– A. N. Wilson

'One of the greatest writers of the twentieth century . . . Simenon was unequalled at making us look inside, though the ability was masked by his brilliance at absorbing us obsessively in his stories'
– *Guardian*

'A novelist who entered his fictional world as if he were part of it'
– Peter Ackroyd

'The greatest of all, the most genuine novelist we have had in literature'
– André Gide

'Superb . . . The most addictive of writers . . . A unique teller of tales'
– *Observer*

'The mysteries of the human personality are revealed in all their disconcerting complexity'
– Anita Brookner

'A writer who, more than any other crime novelist, combined a high literary reputation with popular appeal'
– P. D. James

'A supreme writer . . . Unforgettable vividness'
– *Independent*

'Compelling, remorseless, brilliant'
– John Gray

'Extraordinary masterpieces of the twentieth century'
– John Banville

ABOUT THE AUTHOR

Georges Simenon was born on 12 February 1903 in Liège, Belgium, and died in 1989 in Lausanne, Switzerland, where he had lived for the latter part of his life. Between 1931 and 1972 he published seventy-five novels and twenty-eight short stories featuring Inspector Maigret.

Simenon always resisted identifying himself with his famous literary character, but acknowledged that they shared an important characteristic:

> My motto, to the extent that I have one, has been noted often enough, and I've always conformed to it. It's the one I've given to old Maigret, who resembles me in certain points . . . 'understand and judge not'.

Penguin is publishing the entire series of Maigret novels.

GEORGES SIMENON

Maigret's Childhood Friend

Translated by SHAUN WHITESIDE

PENGUIN BOOKS

PENGUIN CLASSICS

UK | USA | Canada | Ireland | Australia
India | New Zealand | South Africa

Penguin Books is part of the Penguin Random House group of companies
whose addresses can be found at global.penguinrandomhouse.com.

First published in serial, as *L'Ami d'enfance de Maigret*, in *Le Figaro* 1968
First published in book form by Presses de la Cité 1968
This translation first published 2019

002

Copyright © Georges Simenon Limited, 1968
Translation copyright © Shaun Whiteside, 2019
GEORGES SIMENON ® Simenon.tm
MAIGRET ® Georges Simenon Limited
All rights reserved

The moral rights of the author and translator have been asserted

Set in 12.5/15 pt Dante MT Std
Typeset by Jouve (UK), Milton Keynes
Printed and bound in Great Britain by Clays Ltd, Elcograf S.p.A.

ISBN: 978–0–241–30423–5

www.greenpenguin.co.uk

MIX
Paper from
responsible sources
FSC® C018179

Penguin Random House is committed to a
sustainable future for our business, our readers
and our planet. This book is made from Forest
Stewardship Council® certified paper.

Maigret's Childhood Friend

1.

The fly buzzed around his head three times before settling on the top left-hand corner of the page of the report that he was annotating.

The pencil in Maigret's hand came to a standstill, and he looked at the insect with amused curiosity. The game had been going on for almost half an hour, and it was still the same fly. He could have sworn he recognized it. And anyway, it was the only one in the office.

It traced a number of circles in the room, particularly in the area bathed in sunlight, flew around the detective chief inspector's head and landed on the documents that he was studying. There, it lazily rubbed its feet together; it was possible that it was taunting him.

Was it really looking at him? And if it was, what did it make of that mass of flesh, which must have seemed enormous?

He avoided startling it. He waited, pencil in the air, and all of a sudden, as if it had had enough, it took flight and passed through the open window before losing itself in the warm air outside.

It was mid-June. Every now and again a breeze blew through the office where Maigret, in shirt-sleeves, was peacefully smoking his pipe. He had decided to devote the afternoon to reading his inspectors' reports and he did so with all the necessary patience.

It was a curious coincidence. That sun, those cooler gusts that sometimes entered through the open window, that fly that fascinated him reminded him of his years at school, when a fly gravitating towards his desk assumed much more importance than the teacher's lesson.

Joseph, the old usher, knocked discreetly at the door, came in and handed Maigret an embossed visiting card.

Léon Florentin
Antiques Dealer

'How old is he?'

'About your age.'

'Is he tall and thin?'

'Very tall and very thin, yes, with a lot of grey hair.'

It was definitely his Florentin, a fellow pupil of his at the Lycée Banville, in Moulins, where he had been the class joker.

'Show him in.'

He had forgotten the fly, which, perhaps offended, must have flown out the window. There was an awkward moment when Florentin came in, because the two men had only seen each other once since parting company in Moulins. That had been about twenty years ago. Maigret had found himself standing face to face, on the pavement, with an elegant couple. The woman was pretty, very Parisian.

'Let me introduce an old school friend who joined the police.'

Then, to Maigret:

'Allow me to . . .' he began formally, then corrected himself. 'This is Monique, my wife.'

It had been sunny that day too. They hadn't known what to say to each other.

'So, are you well? Still content with life?'

'Still content,' Maigret had replied. 'And you?'

'Can't complain.'

'Do you live in Paris?'

'Yes, 62, Boulevard Haussmann. But I travel a lot for business. I'm just back from Istanbul. You must come and visit us. With Madame Maigret, of course, if you're married . . .'

Neither of them was at ease. The couple had made their way towards an apple-green convertible sports car, and Maigret had continued on his way.

The Florentin who came into his office was less dashing than the one from Place de la Madeleine. He wore quite a tired grey suit and was no longer as self-confident as before.

'It's nice of you to see me straight away. How are you? How are you doing?'

He hesitated to address Maigret informally, and the inspector also struggled to adopt a familiar tone after such a long time.

'And you? Sit down. How's your wife?'

Florentin's light-grey eyes stared into the distance for a moment, as if he was trying to remember.

'You mean Monique, a little redhead? In fact, we lived together for a little while, but I never married her. A nice girl . . .'

'So you aren't married?'

'What's the point?'

And Florentin pulled one of those faces which had once amused his classmates so much and disarmed the teachers. It was as if his long countenance with its well-formed features was made of rubber, the way he managed to twist it in all directions.

Maigret didn't dare to ask why he had come to see him. He studied him, struggling to believe that so many years had passed.

'Lovely office, by the way. I didn't know you had such nice furniture at the Police Judiciaire.'

'You've become an antiques dealer?'

'If you like. I buy up old furniture and repair it in a little studio I've rented on Boulevard Rochechouart. You know, at the moment almost everybody's an antiques dealer.'

'Are you happy?'

'I can't complain, except that I found myself in an awkward situation this afternoon . . .'

He was so used to acting the fool that his face automatically assumed comical expressions. But his face was still ashen, his eyes anxious.

'That's why I came to see you. It occurred to me that you'd be more likely to understand me than anyone else.'

He took a pack of cigarettes out of his pocket, lit one with long and bony fingers that trembled slightly. Maigret thought he caught a whiff of alcohol.

'In fact I'm in a spot of bother.'

'I'm listening . . .'

'I know. It's hard to explain. I've had a girlfriend for four years . . .'

'Another girlfriend that you live with?'

'Yes and no . . . No . . . Not exactly . . . She lives on Rue Notre-Dame-de-Lorette, near Place Saint-Georges.'

Maigret was surprised by his hesitations and his sidelong glances, given that Florentin had always been so confident and loquacious. At school, Maigret had envied him his ease. He also envied him a little because his father was the best patissier in town, opposite the cathedral. He had even given his name to a nut-based cake that had become a local speciality.

Florentin's pockets had always been filled with money. He could pull pranks in class without being punished, as if he enjoyed special immunity. And when evening came he sometimes went out with girls.

'Tell me.'

'Her name is Josée . . . Or rather, her real name is Joséphine Papet, but she prefers Josée. So do I. She's thirty-four and you wouldn't know it . . .'

Florentin's face was so mobile that it seemed to be twitching.

'It's hard to explain, old man . . .'

He got up and walked towards the window, where his tall body was outlined against the sun.

'It's hot in here . . .' he sighed, wiping his brow.

The fly was no longer there to settle on the corner of the pages spread out in front of the inspector. The sound of cars and buses on Pont Saint-Michel could be heard, sometimes the foghorn of a tug lowering its funnel before passing under the arch.

The black marble clock, the same as in all the offices of

the Police Judiciaire and probably in hundreds of official offices, said it was 5.20.

'I'm not the only one . . .' Florentin managed to say at last.

'The only what?'

'Josée's only boyfriend . . . That's what's hard to explain . . . She's the best girl on earth and I was her lover, her friend and her confidant . . .'

Maigret relit his pipe, trying to be patient. His former classmate came and sat down facing him.

'Did she have a lot of other boyfriends?' he asked at last when the silence had actually gone on for a bit too long.

'Wait till I count them . . . There's Paré . . . One . . . Then Courcel . . . Two . . . Then Victor . . . Three . . . Then a young fellow I've never seen and whom I call the redhead . . . Four.'

'Four lovers who come and see her regularly?'

'Some once, others twice a week.'

'They know there are several of them?'

'Of course not.'

'So that each one is under the illusion that he alone is keeping her?'

The word embarrassed Florentin, who started crumbling the tobacco from a cigarette over the carpet.

'I warned you that it was difficult to understand . . .'

'And where do you come into it?'

'I'm her friend . . . I come running when she's lonely.'

'Do you sleep at Rue Notre-Dame-de-Lorette?'

'Except on the night from Thursday to Friday.'

Maigret said, with no apparent irony, 'Because your place is taken?'

'By Courcel, yes . . . She's known him for ten years. He lives in Rouen and has offices on Boulevard Voltaire . . . It would take too long to explain . . . Do you think I'm despicable?'

'I don't think anyone's despicable.'

'I know that my situation might seem problematic and that most people would judge me harshly . . . I swear that Josée and I love each other . . .'

He suddenly added:

'Or rather we loved each other . . .'

The inspector was struck by the word, and his face went blank.

'Have you two broken up?'

'No.'

'Has she died?'

'Yes.'

'When?'

'This afternoon . . .'

And Florentin turned towards him, tragically, and said rather dramatically:

'I swear it wasn't me . . . You know me . . . It's because you know me and I know you that I came to see you . . .'

They had known each other, in fact, at twelve, at fifteen, at seventeen, but since then they had each taken a different path.

'What did she die of?'

'She was shot.'

'By whom?'

'I don't know.'

'Where did it happen?'

'At her apartment . . . In her room . . .'

'Where were you at that moment?'

He was finding it increasingly hard to avoid his usual formality.

'In the closet.'

'You mean in the apartment?'

'Yes . . . It's happened a few times . . . When someone rang the doorbell, I . . . Do I disgust you? I swear it's not what you think . . . I earn my living . . . I work . . .'

'Try and tell me exactly what happened.'

'Since when?'

'Let's say since midday.'

'We had lunch together. She's a very good cook, and we were both sitting at the window. Like every Wednesday, she wasn't expecting anyone until five thirty or six.'

'Who?'

'His name is François Paré, he's about fifty, a departmental head in the Ministry of Public Works. He's the head of Navigable Waterways. He lives in Versailles.'

'He never turns up early?'

'No.'

'What happened after lunch?'

'We chatted.'

'What was she wearing?'

'A dressing gown. Except when she goes out, she always wears a dressing gown. At about three thirty there was a ring on the doorbell, and I hurried to the wardrobe. It doesn't open on to the bedroom, but on to the bathroom . . .'

Maigret was losing patience.

'And then?'

'Perhaps a quarter of an hour later I heard a sound like a gunshot . . .'

'So at three forty-five . . .?'

'I suppose . . .'

'You ran in?'

'No. I wasn't supposed to be there. And anyway, what I had taken for a gunshot might have come from the exhaust of a car or a bus.'

Maigret was now looking at him with keen interest. He remembered the stories that Florentin had told them in the old days, all of which were more or less fantastical. Sometimes it seemed as if he himself couldn't tell lies from the truth.

'And what were you waiting for?'

'You're addressing me formally now? You can see that . . .'

He looked troubled and disappointed.

'Fine! What were you waiting for, in the closet?' He had softened his tone.

'It's not a closet, it's quite a large wardrobe. I was waiting for the man to leave.'

'How do you know it was a man, when you didn't see him?'

Florentin gave him a baffled look.

'I hadn't thought of that.'

'Did this Josée have no women friends?'

'No.'

'No family?'

'She's originally from Concarneau, and I've never seen any of her family.'

'How did you know the person had left?'

'I heard footsteps in the sitting room, then the door opened and closed again.'

'At what time?'

'About four.'

'So the murderer stayed with his victim for a quarter of an hour?'

'It looks that way.'

'When you stepped into the room, where did you find your mistress?'

'On the floor, beside the bed.'

'What was she wearing?'

'She was still in her yellow dressing gown.'

'Where had she been shot?'

'In the throat.'

'Are you sure she was dead?'

'It wasn't hard to tell.'

'Was the room untidy?'

'I didn't notice.'

'No open drawers, scattered papers?'

'No . . . I don't think so . . .'

'You're not sure?'

'I was too shocked.'

'Did you call a doctor?'

'No . . . Given that she was dead . . .'

'The local police station?'

'Not them either.'

'You got here just after five. What had you been doing since four o'clock?'

'First of all, I collapsed into an armchair, in a complete

daze . . . I didn't understand . . . I still don't understand . . . Then I told myself that I would be accused, especially since our poisonous old concierge hates me.'

'So you stayed in that armchair for an hour?'

'No . . . I don't know how long afterwards I went out to the bistro, the Grand Saint-Georges, where I had three brandies one after the other.'

'And after that?'

'I remembered that you had become the big chief of the Crime Squad.'

'How did you get here?'

'I took a taxi.'

Maigret was furious, but his face was so frozen that it was impossible to tell. He went and opened the door of the inspectors' office and hesitated between Janvier and Lapointe, who were both there. In the end he chose Janvier.

'Come here a moment . . . First call Moers at the lab and tell him to meet us at Rue Notre-Dame-de-Lorette . . . What number?'

'17A.'

Every time he looked at his old schoolmate he wore the same hard and closed expression. While Janvier made his call he glanced at the clock, which said it was 5.30.

'Who is the Wednesday client again?'

'Paré . . . The man from the ministry.'

'Normally, at this time of day, he would be turning up at the door to the apartment?'

'This is the time, yes.'

'Has he got a key?'

'None of them has a key.'

'Not even you?'

'I'm different . . . You see, old man—'

'I would rather you didn't call me "old man".'

'You see! Even you . . .'

'Let's get going.'

He picked up his hat in passing and, as they walked down the wide greyish staircase, he stuffed a pipe.

'I wonder why you waited so long to come and see me, or to alert the police . . . Did she have a lot of money?'

'I suppose so . . . Three or four years ago, as a stopgap, she bought a house on Rue du Mont-Cenis, just above Montmartre.'

'Was there any money in the apartment?'

'It's possible . . . I couldn't swear to it . . . What I do know is that she was suspicious of banks.'

They chose one of the little black cars lined up in the courtyard, and Janvier sat down at the wheel.

'Are you trying to make me believe that, even though you were living with her, you didn't know where she kept her savings?'

'It's the truth.'

He wanted to say: 'Stop acting the clown.'

Did he feel sorry for him?

'How many rooms are there in the apartment?'

'There's a sitting room, a dining room, an en-suite bed-room and a small kitchen.'

'Not counting the wardrobe.'

'Not counting the wardrobe.'

Slipping between the other cars, Janvier tried to work

out what they were talking about from the few retorts exchanged.

'I swear, Maigret . . .'

And he still didn't call him Jules, because at school they always called one another by their surnames.

As the three men passed in front of the lodge, Maigret noticed the tulle curtain of the glass door moving and, behind it, a huge and bulky concierge. Her face matched her body and, blank-faced, she stared at them as fixedly as a life-sized portrait or a statue.

The lift was cramped, and Maigret found himself pressed up against Florentin, his eyes very close to those of his old schoolmate, and he felt awkward. What was the son of the Moulins patissier thinking about right now? Was it fear that made him grimace constantly, even though he attempted to assume a natural expression, or even to smile?

Was he Joséphine Papet's murderer? What had he done for an hour before showing up at Quai des Orfèvres?

They crossed the third-floor landing, and Florentin quite naturally took a bunch of keys from his pocket. After a tiny hallway, they entered a sitting room where Maigret thought he had gone back fifty years in time, if not more. The old rose silk curtains were draped as in those days, and held by tie-backs of thick braided silk. On the parquet floor, a carpet with faded colours. Plush and silk everywhere, and doilies, squares of embroidery or lace on fake Louis XVI armchairs.

Near the window, a sofa covered with velvet, with a

multitude of cushions that were still crumpled as if some-one had just sat down on them. A pedestal table. A lamp with a pink shade on a gilded stand.

This must have been Josée's favourite corner. She had a record player within reach, chocolates, magazines and several romantic novels. The television was just opposite her, on the other side of the room.

On the wallpaper, patterned with little flowers, a number of canvases hung, showing highly detailed landscapes.

Florentin, who was reading Maigret's expression, con-firmed what he was thinking:

'That was where she sat most often.'

'What about you?'

The antiques dealer pointed to an old leather armchair that clashed with the rest of the furniture.

'I bought that for her.'

The dining room was just as old-fashioned, just as banal, just as stuffy, and here too there were velvet cur-tains, with pot plants on both window-sills.

The door to the bedroom was half open. Florentin was reluctant to go through it. Maigret went in first and, less than two metres away, saw the body lying on the carpet. As is often the case, the hole in the throat looked larger than the calibre of a bullet. She had lost a lot of blood, and yet her face showed nothing but astonishment.

As far as he could tell, the woman was short, plump and gentle, one of those women who make you think of well-cooked stews, of lovingly potted jams.

Maigret looked around for something.

'I haven't seen a weapon,' his schoolmate announced, having guessed. 'Unless she fell on it, which strikes me as unlikely.'

The telephone was in the sitting room. Maigret decided to get the indispensable formalities out of the way.

'Janvier, phone the local station first of all. Ask the inspector to bring a doctor. Then let the prosecutor's office know.'

Moers' forensic team arrived a few moments later. Maigret had hoped to take a few minutes to carry out an initial inspection in peace. He went into the bathroom, where the towels were pink. There was a lot of pink in the apartment. When he opened the door of the wardrobe, which consisted of a kind of corridor leading nowhere, he found more pink, the candy pink of a bed-jacket, the brighter pink of a summer dress. The other clothes were also in pastel colours, apple green, pale blue.

'You don't have any suits here?'

'It would be difficult . . .' Florentin murmured, slightly awkwardly. 'As far as the others are concerned, she's supposed to live on her own.'

Obviously! That was old-fashioned too: these mature men who came once or twice a week, living under the illusion that they were keeping a mistress, while remaining unaware of one another.

But were they really all unaware of one another?

Back in the bedroom, Maigret opened drawers, found invoices, underwear, a case containing a few inexpensive jewels.

It was six o'clock.

'The Wednesday gentleman should have arrived by now,' he observed.

'Perhaps he came upstairs and, when he rang the bell and got no answer, he left again?'

Janvier announced:

'The inspector is on the way. The deputy prosecutor will be here any minute, with an examining magistrate.'

This was the point in an investigation that Maigret hated most. Five or six of them stood looking at each other, then looking at the body with the doctor kneeling next to it. A pure formality. The doctor could only confirm the death, and the details would come only after the post-mortem. The deputy prosecutor also took note, on behalf of the government.

The examining magistrate looked at Maigret as if asking him what he thought, when he didn't yet think anything. As to the police chief, he was in a hurry to get back to his office.

'Keep me up to date,' murmured the magistrate, who was about forty and must have been new to Paris.

His name was Page. He had risen through the ranks, starting with a sub-prefecture and then passing through a succession of increasingly large cities.

Moers and his men were waiting in the drawing room, where one of the experts was looking around for fingerprints.

When the officers had left, Maigret said to them:

'Your turn, boys . . . First some photographs of the victim, before the van comes to get her.'

When he headed towards the door, Florentin wanted to follow him.

'No. You stay here. You, Janvier, question the neighbours on the landing and, if necessary, the ones on the floor upstairs, to find out if they heard anything.'

Maigret went downstairs. The house was old-fashioned, but still very presentable. The crimson carpet was fixed to each step with brass bars. Almost all the door-handles were polished, as was a plaque that announced: 'Mademoiselle Vial, corsets and girdles made to measure'.

He found the monumental concierge at her door, behind the curtain, which she held aside with sausage-like fingers. When he made as if to enter, she took a step back, almost without moving, and he pushed the door open.

She looked at him as indifferently as if he were some random object and didn't flinch when he showed her his Police Judiciaire detective chief inspector's badge.

'I don't suppose you've heard?'

She didn't open her mouth, but her eyes seemed to say, 'Heard what?'

The lodge was clean, with a circular table in the middle and two canaries in a cage. A kitchen could be seen in the background.

'Mademoiselle Papet is dead.'

She spoke at last. For she could indeed speak, in a slightly faint voice that displayed the same indifference as her expression. Or was it hostility rather than indifference? She looked at the world through her door and hated it, all of it.

'Is that why there was all that noise on the stairs? There are at least ten of them up there, isn't that right?'

'What's your name?'

'I don't see why my name should be of interest to you.'

'Because I have a certain number of questions to ask you, I have to mention your name in my report.'

'Madame Blanc.'

'Are you a widow?'

'No.'

'Does your husband live here?'

'No.'

'Did he leave you?'

'Nineteen years ago.'

At last she sat down on an enormous armchair that matched her size, and Maigret sat down too.

'Did anyone go up to Mademoiselle Papet's between five thirty and six o'clock?'

'Yes. At five forty.'

'Who?'

'The Wednesday one, of course. I've never asked them their names. A tall man, thinning hair, always wears dark colours.'

'Did he stay up there for long?'

'No.'

'He didn't speak to you when he came back down?'

'He asked me if the Papet woman had gone out.'

He had to drag the words out of her one by one.

'What did you say?'

'That I hadn't seen her.'

'Did he seem surprised?'

'Yes.'

It was tiring, particularly since her facial expression was as motionless as her obese body.

'You didn't see him earlier in the afternoon?'

'No.'

'At about three thirty, for example, you didn't see any-one go upstairs? Were you here?'

'I was here and no one went upstairs.'

'No one came down either? At about four o'clock?'

'Only at twenty past four.'

'Who?'

'That guy . . .'

'Who do you mean by "that guy"?'

'The one who arrived with you. I'd rather not call that guy anything else.'

'Joséphine Papet's live-in lover?'

She smiled with bitter irony.

'He hasn't talked to you?'

'I wouldn't even have opened the door to him.'

'Are you sure that no one else went upstairs or down-stairs between three thirty and four thirty?'

Having said it once, she didn't take the time to repeat herself.

'Do you know your tenant's other friends?'

'Why do you call them friends?'

'Her other visitors . . . How many of them are there?'

She moved her lips as if murmuring prayers in church and said at last:

'Four. Apart from him.'

'There were never any unpleasant encounters between them?'

'Not to my knowledge.'

'You spend the whole day in that room?'

'Except in the morning, when I do the shopping, and then when I clean the stairs.'

'No one came to keep you company today?'

'No one ever comes to keep me company.'

'Did Mademoiselle Papet ever go out?'

'At about eleven o'clock in the morning, to go shopping. She didn't go far. Sometimes, in the evening, she went to the cinema with the guy.'

'And on Sunday?'

'Sometimes they went out in a car.'

'Whose is the car?'

'Hers, of course.'

'And who drives?'

'He does.'

'Do you know where the car is?'

'In a garage on Rue La Bruyère.'

She didn't ask him what her tenant had died of. She had as little curiosity as she had energy, and Maigret looked at her with mounting bewilderment.

'Mademoiselle Papet was murdered.'

'That was to be expected, wasn't it?'

'Why?'

'With all those men . . .'

'She was killed by a bullet fired almost point-blank.'

She listened without a word.

'She never confided in you?'

'We weren't friends.'

'Did you hate her?'

'That's not it either.'

In the end it was becoming oppressive, and Maigret

wiped his brow, left the lodge and was happy to be back on the pavement. The van from the Forensic Institute had just arrived. The men would take out the stretcher, and he preferred to cross the street and go into the Grand Saint-Georges, where he ordered a beer at the counter.

The murder of Joséphine Papet hadn't caused a stir in the area, not even in the house where she had lived for many years.

He saw the van driving away. When he went back into the house, the concierge was at her post, and she looked at him just as she had done the first time. He took the lift and rang the doorbell. Janvier opened up.

'Have you questioned the neighbours?'

'The ones I was able to find. There are only two apartments to the front, on each floor, and only one overlooking the courtyard. Next door I found a certain Madame Sauveur, a middle-aged woman, very pleasant, very elegant. She stayed at home all afternoon, listening to the radio and knitting.

'She did hear a noise, like a muffled explosion, around mid-afternoon, and she thought it was a car or bus backfiring.'

'She didn't hear the door opening and closing again?'

'I checked. You can't hear from her apartment. The building is quite old, and the walls are thick.'

'On the fourth floor?'

'A couple with two children went off to the country or the seaside a week ago. To the back there's a retired railwayman who lives with his grandson. He didn't hear anything.'

Florentin was standing by the open window.

'Was it already open this afternoon?' Maigret asked him.

'I think so . . . Yes . . .'

'And the bedroom window?'

'Definitely not.'

'How can you be so sure?'

'Because Josée was always careful to close it again when she had a visitor.'

Opposite, four or five girls could be seen sewing in a studio where a mannequin covered in coarse cloth stood on a black wooden stand.

Florentin looked worried, even though he always made an effort to keep a smile on his face. It gave him a strange rictus that reminded Maigret of the Lycée Banville, when his classmate got caught by the teacher he was imitating behind his back.

'Do you enjoy reminding us of our origins, Monsieur Florentin?' the little, pale, fair-haired man who taught them Latin used to say in those days.

Moers' colleagues went through the apartment with a fine-tooth comb, and nothing, not so much as a speck of dust, escaped their attention. In spite of the open window, Maigret was hot. He didn't like this business, which repelled him slightly. He also hated finding himself in an awkward situation. In spite of himself, images of the past appeared in his mind.

He knew practically nothing of what had become of his former fellow-pupils, and the one who had made a sudden reappearance was in a more than delicate position.

'Have you talked to the war memorial?'

Maigret looked at Florentin in surprise.

'The concierge. That's what I call her. I bet she's got a pretty harsh name for me.'

' "That guy" . . .'

'Right! I'm that guy. What did she say to you?'

'Are you sure you've told me the facts as they happened?'

'Why would I have lied to you?'

'You've always lied. You used to lie for fun.'

'That was forty years ago!'

'You don't seem to have changed that much.'

'If I'd had something to hide from you, would I have gone to see you?'

'What else could you have done?'

'Gone away. Gone back to my place on Boulevard Rochechouart.'

'To be arrested tomorrow morning?'

'I could have fled, crossed the border.'

'Have you got any money?'

Florentin blushed, and Maigret felt a little sorry for him. When he was young, his long clownish face, his jokes and grimaces had been amusing.

Now he wasn't funny any more, and it was rather painful to see him resorting to his old face-pulling.

'But you don't think I killed her?'

'Why not?'

'You know me.'

'I last saw you twenty years ago, on Place de la Madeleine, and before that we have to go as far back as the lycée in Moulins.'

'Do I look like a murderer?'

'It takes only a few minutes, a few seconds, to become a murderer. Before that you're a man like any other.'

'Why would I have killed her? We were the best friends in the world.'

'Just friends?'

'Of course not, but at my age I'm not going to make out it was some sort of grand passion.'

'And she was the same?'

'I think she loved me.'

'Was she jealous?'

'I gave her no reason to be . . . You still haven't told me what the witch downstairs told you.'

Janvier looked at his boss with a certain curiosity, because it was probably the first time that he had seen an interrogation play out in such conditions. Maigret was obviously uneasy, hesitating, just as he hesitated at every moment between familiarity and formality.

'She didn't see anyone go upstairs.'

'She's lying. Either that or she was in her kitchen.'

'She claims not to have left the lodge.'

'That's impossible, for heaven's sake! The killer had to come from somewhere . . . Unless . . .'

'Unless what?'

'He was already in the building . . .'

'A tenant?'

Florentin quickly pounced on that hypothesis.

'Why not? I'm not the only man in the block.'

'Did Josée socialize with some of the tenants?'

'How could I know? I'm not always here. I've got a job. I have to earn my living.'

It sounded fake. Another bit of play-acting on the part of Florentin, who had been play-acting all his life.

'Janvier, I want you to examine the building from top to bottom, knock on all the doors, question everyone you can find. I'm going back to headquarters.'

'What about the car?'

Because Maigret had never wanted to learn to drive.

'I'll take a taxi.'

And to Florentin:

'Come on.'

'You don't intend to arrest me?'

'No.'

'What are you going to do? Why do you need me?'

'To have a chat.'

2.

Maigret's first idea had been to go with his companion to Quai des Orfèvres, but as he leaned forward towards the driver he changed his mind.

'What number Boulevard Rochechouart?' he asked Florentin.

'55A . . . Why?'

'55A, Boulevard Rochechouart.'

It was no distance away. The driver, annoyed to have been stopped for such a short trip, muttered between his teeth.

On one side there was a picture-framer, on the other a tobacconist. Between the two, a cul-de-sac with uneven cobblestones, with a handcart parked in it. At the end, two studios with large windows. In the one on the left, a painter was busy painting a view of Sacré-Coeur which he would probably sell to a tourist. It looked as if he mass-produced them. He had long hair, a salt-and-pepper beard and a floppy neck-tie like the Montmartre artists of the turn of the century.

Florentin pulled his keys from his pocket and opened the door of the studio on the right, and Maigret was angry with him for spoiling his childhood memories.

What had become of the other boys in his class? He hadn't seen any of them again. Crochet, the son of a notary, must have followed in his father's footsteps. Orban, gentle and podgy, talked about studying medicine. Others must have scattered and settled elsewhere in France and abroad.

Why did it have to be Florentin, of all people, that he met up with again in such unpleasant circumstances?

He remembered the patisserie, even though he hadn't gone in often. Other pupils, who had more pocket money, met there for ice cream and cake, in a setting of mirrors, marble and gilt, a warm, sweet atmosphere. For the ladies of the town, a cake was only any good if it came from Florentin's.

Now he found himself in a dusty junk shop, and the windows, which had probably never been washed, allowed in only a faint light.

'Apologies for the mess.'

The term 'antiques dealer', in fact, was more than just pretentious. The items of furniture that Florentin bought, God knows where, were mostly old things without style or value. He merely repaired them and sanded them to give them a slightly more attractive appearance.

'Have you been doing this job for a long time?'

'Three years.'

'And before that?'

'I worked in exports.'

'Exporting what?'

'Pretty much everything. Mostly to the countries of sub-Saharan Africa.'

'And before that?'

Then Florentin, humiliated, murmured:

'You know, I tried pretty much everything. I didn't want to be a pastry-chef and end my days in Moulins. My sister married a pastry-chef, and they carried on the business.'

Maigret remembered the sister with the well-filled blouse who stood behind the white counter. Hadn't he been slightly in love with her? She was fresh and cheerful, like her mother, whom she resembled.

'In Paris, it isn't easy to hold your own. I've had my ups and downs . . .'

Maigret had known others who had had highs and lows, who had set up lucrative businesses that collapsed like houses of cards, and who were constantly on the brink of jail. People who ask you for a limited partnership of a hundred thousand francs to build a harbour in a faraway country and who settle in the end for a hundred francs so as not to be thrown out of their apartment.

Florentin had found Josée. Looking at the studio, it was plain that Florentin didn't live by selling furniture.

Maigret pushed a half-open door and revealed a cramped, windowless room containing an iron bed, a wash-stand and a rickety wardrobe.

'Is this where you sleep?'

'Only on Thursdays.'

Who did Thursday belong to again? The only one who spent the night once a week at Rue Notre-Dame-de-Lorette.

'Fernand Courcel,' Florentin explained. 'He was Josée's friend before I was. As long as ten years ago he came to see her and they went out together. He's less free now, but on Thursday evening he has an excuse to stay in Paris.'

Maigret peered in the corners, opened drawers, old unremarkable wardrobes whose varnish had faded. He couldn't have said exactly what he was looking for. One detail bothered him.

'You told me that Josée had no bank account?'

'Yes. At least not to my knowledge.'

'Was she suspicious of banks?'

'That's part of it. Mostly, she didn't want anyone to know about her income, because of taxes.'

Maigret spotted an old pipe.

'Do you smoke a pipe these days?'

'Not at her place. She didn't like the smell. Only here.'

A blue suit hung in a rustic wardrobe, along with some work trousers. Some shirts, three or four, and, apart from a pair of sawdust-covered espadrilles, one pair of shoes.

A scruffy bohemian. Joséphine Papet must have had money. Was she miserly? Was she suspicious of Florentin, who would have taken her for everything she had?

He couldn't find anything interesting and was almost sorry to have come, because in the end he felt sorry for his former classmate. From the doorway he thought he could see a piece of paper on top of a wardrobe. He turned on his heels, climbed on a chair and stepped down holding a rectangular package wrapped in newspaper.

Sweat glistened on Florentin's forehead.

Having unfolded the newspaper, Maigret revealed a white biscuit tin with the trademark still visible in red and yellow. When he opened it, he found rolls of hundred-franc notes.

'Those are my savings . . .'

The inspector looked at him as if he hadn't heard him and sat down at the workbench to count the rolls. There were forty-eight.

'Do you often eat biscuits?'

'Sometimes.'

'Can you show me another tin?'

'I don't think I have any at the moment.'

'I've seen two of the same brand at Rue Notre-Dame-de-Lorette.'

'That's probably where I got it.'

He had always lied, instinctively or for fun. He needed to tell stories, and the more unlikely they were the cheekier he became. Except this time there was a lot at stake.

'I understand why you didn't get to Quai des Orfèvres until five o'clock.'

'I held back . . . I was worried that I would be accused . . .'

'You came here.'

He denied it again, but he was starting to get rattled.

'Do you want me to go and ask the painter next door?'

'Listen, Maigret . . .'

His lip was trembling. It looked as if he was going to cry, and it wasn't a pleasant sight.

'I know I don't always tell the truth. It's stronger than me. You remember the stories I made up to amuse you . . . Today, I beg you to believe me: I wasn't the one who killed Josée and I was in the wardrobe when it happened . . .'

His expression was melodramatic, but then again wasn't he used to acting?

'If I had killed somebody, I wouldn't have come to you.'

'So why didn't you confess the truth to me?'

'What truth?'

He was playing for time. He was hedging his bets.

'At three o'clock, this afternoon, the white tin was still in Rue Notre-Dame-de-Lorette. Is that right?'

'Yes.'

'So?'

'It's easy to understand . . . Josée had no relationship with her family. Her only sister is in Morocco, where her husband grows citrus fruits. They're rich. I'm hanging on by my fingernails. So, when I realized that she was dead . . .'

'You took advantage of the situation to walk off with the loot.'

'That's putting it crudely, but I can see it from your point of view. Once and for all, I didn't hurt anyone. What was going to become of me without her?'

Maigret stared at him, tugged in different directions by contradictory emotions.

'Come with me.'

He was hot. He was thirsty. He felt tired, dissatisfied with himself and everyone else.

Leaving the courtyard, he paused, before at last pushing his former classmate into the bar.

'Two beers,' he ordered.

'Do you believe me?'

'We'll talk again later.'

Maigret had two beers and then went to look for a taxi. It was rush hour, and it took them almost half an hour to get to the Police Judiciaire. The sky was a solid, heavy blue, the café tables were full, and a lot of men could be seen in shirt-sleeves with their jackets under their arms.

His office was quite cool, because the sun was no longer shining into it.

'Sit down. You can smoke if you like.'

'Thank you. You know, it feels strange, finding myself face to face with somebody I was at school with.'

'Me too,' Maigret muttered, stuffing his pipe.

'It's not the same.'

'True enough.'

'You're judging me harshly, aren't you! You must think I'm a scoundrel.'

'I'm not judging you. I'm trying to understand.'

'I loved her.'

'Ah!'

'I'm not claiming it was a grand romance, or that we thought we were Romeo and Juliet . . .'

'I can't actually imagine Romeo waiting in the wardrobe. Has that happened to you often?'

'Only three or four times, when someone turned up unexpectedly.'

'Were these gentlemen aware of your existence?'

'Of course not.'

'You never met them?'

'I saw them. I wanted to know what they looked like and I waited for them in the street. You can see that I'm talking to you openly.'

'You weren't tempted to blackmail them? I assume they're married, they have children.'

'I swear . . .'

'Would you stop swearing?'

'Fine. But what can I tell you, since you don't believe me?'

'The truth.'

'I've never blackmailed anybody.'

'Why?'

'I'd settled on our little life. I'm not as young as I was. I've been around long enough to want some peace and security. Josée was calming and she saw to my every need.'

'Was it you who suggested that she buy a car?'

'We thought about it together. Maybe I mentioned it first.'

'Where did you go on Sundays?'

'Anywhere, the Chevreuse valley, the forest of Fontainebleau, sometimes, more rarely, to the seaside.'

'You knew where she kept her money?'

'She didn't hide it from me. She trusted me completely . . . Tell me, Maigret, why would I have killed her?'

'Supposing she'd tired of you.'

'That's the opposite of what happened. If she saved money, it was so that one day we could go and live in the countryside together. Put yourself in my place . . .'

In spite of himself, Maigret pulled a face.

'Did you own a revolver?'

'There was an old revolver in the bedside table. I found it over two years ago in a piece of furniture that I'd bought at auction.'

'With its cartridges?'

'It was loaded, yes.'

'And you brought it to Rue Notre-Dame-de-Lorette?'

'Josée was quite fearful and, to reassure her, I put the gun in the bedside table.'

'That weapon has disappeared.'

'I know. I've looked for it too.'

'Why?'

'It's stupid, I realize. Everything I do, everything I say is stupid. I'm too frank. I would have been better off calling the local station and waiting. I could have told them anything at all, that I'd just turned up and found her dead . . .'

'I asked you a question. Why did you look for the revolver?'

'To get rid of it. I would have thrown it in the sewer, or in the Seine. The simple fact that it belonged to me meant that they were obviously going to accuse me. And you can see that I was right, because even you . . .'

'I haven't accused you yet.'

'But you brought me here and you don't believe what I'm saying to you . . . Am I under arrest?'

Maigret looked at him hesitantly. He was serious and worried.

'No,' he said at last.

He was taking a risk, he knew, but he didn't feel brave enough to act otherwise.

'What are you going to do when you get out of here?'

'I'll have to have a bite to eat, I suppose. Then I'll go to bed.'

'Where?'

Florentin hesitated.

'I don't know . . . I suppose it's better if I don't go to Rue Notre-Dame-de-Lorette . . .'

Was it a lack of awareness?

'I'll probably have to sleep at Boulevard Rochechouart.'

In the windowless storeroom at the end of the studio, in a bed that didn't even have any sheets, only a rough old grey blanket.

Maigret got up and stepped into the inspectors' office. He waited behind Lapointe until he had finished speaking on the phone.

'I've got somebody in my office, a tall, thin fellow. He's my age, and he's in poor shape. He lives at the end of a courtyard, at 55A, Boulevard Rochechouart. I don't know what he's going to do, where he will go when he leaves here. I'd like you not to let him out of your sight.

'For the night, arrange something with a colleague. And someone else to take over tomorrow morning.'

'He mustn't know he's being tailed?'

'It would be better if he didn't notice, but that's not hugely important. He's as sly as a fox and he's bound to suspect it.'

'Fine, chief. I'll wait for him in the corridor.'

'I'll only be with him for a few more minutes.'

When Maigret pushed the door open, Florentin started abruptly, trying to regain his composure.

'Were you listening?'

The other man hesitated and finally stretched his wide mouth into quite a pitiful smile.

'What would you have done in my place?'

'Did you hear?'

'Not everything.'

'One of my inspectors is going to follow you. If you try and give him the slip, I should warn you that I'll send your description to the whole police force and have you arrested.'

'Why are you talking to me like this, Maigret?'

The inspector almost asked him to stop calling him by his surname, and to stop being so familiar with him. He didn't have the stomach for it.

'Where were you planning to go?'

'When?'

'You believed that there would be an investigation, that you'd fall under suspicion. The fact that you hid the money so badly is because you haven't had time to find anywhere to stash it securely. Were you already planning to come and see me?'

'No. First of all I intended to go to the station.'

'Not to leave France before the body was discovered?'

'Just for a moment . . .'

'What stopped you?'

'My flight would have been taken as proof of my guilt, and I would have been extradited. Then I had the idea of going to the local station, and then all of a sudden I remembered you. I've often seen your name in the papers. You're the only one in the whole class to have become almost famous.'

Maigret was still looking at him with the same curiosity, as if his former classmate presented him with an insoluble problem.

'They say you don't trust appearances, and that you get to the bottom of things. So I hoped you would understand . . . I'm starting to wonder if I wasn't mistaken . . . Admit it, you believe that I'm guilty . . .'

'I've already told you I don't believe anything.'

'I shouldn't have taken the money. It only occurred to me at the last minute, when I was already at the door.'

'You can go.'

They were both standing up, and Florentin was reluctant to extend his hand. Perhaps to avoid the handshake, Maigret took his handkerchief from his pocket and wiped his brow.

'Will I see you tomorrow?'

'That's quite likely.'

'Goodbye, Maigret.'

'Goodbye.'

He didn't watch him go down the stairs with Lapointe on his heels.

For no precise reason, Maigret was displeased with him. Not with himself or anyone else. Someone had spoiled a day which had, until five in the afternoon, been pleasant and idle.

The files were still on his desk, waiting for him to pay attention to them and annotate them. The fly had disappeared, perhaps upset that he hadn't turned up for their appointment.

It was 7.30. He called his apartment on Boulevard Richard-Lenoir.

'Is that you?'

An odd habit, because he had easily recognized his wife's voice.

'Aren't you coming home for dinner?'

She was so used to it that it was her first reflex when he called.

'As it happens, I'm on my way. What are we having? . . . Fine . . . Fine . . . I'll see you in about half an hour.'

He stepped into the inspectors' office, where only a few

members of the team were left, sat down at Janvier's desk and wrote a note asking him to call him as soon as he got back.

He still felt slightly uneasy. This was no ordinary case, and the fact that Florentin was a kind of childhood friend didn't make it any better. Then there were the others, middle-aged men occupying more or less important positions. Each of them led calm and regular lives in the bosom of their families.

Except one day a week! Except for the few hours that they spent in Joséphine Papet's hushed apartment.

Tomorrow morning the papers would get hold of the story, and they would start trembling.

He needed to go up under the eaves, to the offices of Criminal Records, to ask Moers if any results had come in. In the end he shrugged and took his hat off the hook.

'See you tomorrow, boys.'

'See you tomorrow, chief.'

He walked through the crowd to Châtelet and joined the queue to wait for his bus.

As soon as she saw him, Madame Maigret knew that he was out of sorts, and she looked quizzically at him in spite of herself.

'An irritating business,' he growled, going to the bathroom to wash his hands.

Then he took off his jacket and loosened his tie a little.

'A former schoolmate who's up to his neck in an impossible situation. Not to mention the fact that no one is going to feel remotely sympathetic to him.'

'A murder?'

'Gunshot. The woman is dead.'

'Jealousy?'

'No. He wasn't the one who fired the gun.'

'They're not sure it was him?'

'Let's eat,' he sighed, as if he had talked about the case too much already.

All the windows were open, the light gilded by the setting sun. Madame Maigret had made the chicken with tarragon that she cooked so well and served it with asparagus tips.

She was wearing a cotton dress with little flowers of the kind that she liked to wear when she stayed indoors, and that added an extra feeling of intimacy to the dinner.

'Do you have to go out tonight?'

'I don't think so. I'm waiting for a call from Janvier.'

The phone rang just as he was about to plunge his spoon into his melon.

'Hello, yes . . . I'm listening, Janvier . . . Are you back at the office? . . . Have you dug up anything?'

'Hardly anything, chief. First of all, I questioned the two shopkeepers on the ground floor. On the left there's a lingerie shop, Chez Éliane. The kind of lingerie that you can only get in Montmartre. Apparently the tourists are wild about it.

'The two girls, one fair and one dark, follow the comings and goings in the building more or less closely. They immediately recognized my description of Florentin and the dead woman. She was a customer, even though she didn't care for fancy lingerie.

'Apparently she was a charming woman, calm and with a ready smile, like a nice, neatly dressed, respectable housewife.

'They knew that Florentin lived with her and they liked him too. They even thought he seemed aristocratic. An aristocrat who had come down in the world, as they say.

'They were a bit cross with Josée for deceiving him, because they'd once seen her coming out with the Wednesday gentleman.'

'François Paré? The one at the Ministry of Public Works?'

'I suppose so. That's how they knew who he was visiting every week, almost always at the same time. He drives a black Citroën and he always has trouble finding a parking space. He always brings a box of pastries.'

'Do they also know the other lovers?'

'Only the Thursday one, the oldest one. He's been coming to Rue Notre-Dame-de-Lorette for years, and they think he lived in the apartment for several weeks a very long time ago. They call him Fatty. He has a babyish face, round and pink, with bright, sensitive eyes.

'Almost every week he would go out with her to have dinner in town, and then probably to go to a show. He must have slept at the apartment afterwards, because he didn't leave again until late morning.'

Maigret consulted his notes.

'That's Fernand Courcel, from Rouen. He has offices in Paris, Boulevard Voltaire . . . The others?'

'They didn't tell me anything about the others, and they're sure it was Florentin who was being deceived.'

'And then?'

'The shop on the right is occupied by Martin's Shoes. It's dark in there, and the shop is set back. The window display keeps you from seeing what's happening in the street, unless you stand behind the glass door.'

'Go on.'

'On the first floor on the left, a dentist. He doesn't know anything. He's been treating Josée for four years. Three visits for a filling. On the right, an old couple who hardly go out any more. The husband worked at the Banque de France, I don't know in what position. Their daughter is married and comes to see them every Sunday with her husband and their two children.

'The apartment overlooking the courtyard: no one at the moment. The tenants have been in Italy for a month. The husband and wife work in catering.

'Second floor. The lady who makes made-to-measure corsets. Two girls work with her. They aren't even aware of Joséphine Papet's existence.

'On the other side of the landing, a woman with three children, the oldest of them only five. Loud voice. Then again you have to shout to be heard above the squealing of the children.

' "It's disgusting," she said to me. "I've written to the owner. My husband didn't want me to, but I did anyway. He's always worried about attracting trouble. You don't practise that profession in a respectable household where there are children. There was one almost every day, and I recognized them by their ring on the doorbell. The one with the limp came early on Saturday, immediately after

43

lunch. It was easy to recognize his footstep. And he also rang the bell in rhythm: ta, ta, ta, ta . . . ta, ta! Poor fool! Maybe he thought he was the only one."'

'You haven't found out anything else about him?'

'Only that he's a man in his fifties and that he comes in a taxi.'

'The redhead?'

'He's new. He's only been visiting the house for a few weeks. He's younger than the others, between thirty and thirty-five, and he climbs the stairs four at a time.'

'Has he got a key?'

'No. No one has a key except Florentin, whom the tenant on the second floor calls a distinguished pimp.

' "I prefer the ones near Place Pigalle," she says. "At least they're taking a risk. And they wouldn't be good for anything else. While a man who must be of good family and who probably has an education . . ."'

Maigret couldn't suppress a smile, sorry not to have questioned the whole household himself.

'On the right, no one answered. On the fourth floor I found myself in the middle of a domestic.

' "If you don't tell me where you went and who you saw . . ." the husband was shouting.

' "I can still go shopping without telling you the names of all the shops I went into, can't I? Or do I need to bring you a shopkeepers' certificate . . .?"

' "You're not going to tell me it takes you a whole afternoon to buy a pair of shoes. Answer my question. Who . . .?"

' "Who what?"

44

' "Who did you meet?"

'I preferred to creep away,' Janvier said by way of conclusion. 'Opposite, an old woman. It's crazy, the number of old women in that part of town. She doesn't know anything. She's half deaf, and her apartment smells of rancid butter.

'On the off chance, I tried the concierge . . . She looked at me with her fish eyes, and I couldn't get anything out of her.'

'Neither did I, if that's any consolation. Except that according to her nobody went upstairs between three and four.'

'Is she sure about that?'

'It's what she claims. She also states that she didn't leave her lodge, and no one could have got past her without her knowledge. She will stubbornly repeat as much, even in court.'

'What do I do now?'

'You go home. I'll see you in the office tomorrow morning.'

'Goodnight, chief.'

Maigret had only just hung up and was about to return to his melon, when the phone rang again. This time it was Lapointe. An excited voice.

'I've been trying to get through to you for a quarter of an hour, but it was always engaged. Before that, I tried headquarters. I'm calling you from the bar on the corner. We've got some news, chief.'

'Tell me.'

'When we left the Police Judiciaire, he knew very well

that I was following him, and as he went down the stairs he even turned round to glance at me.

'On the pavement I followed him at a distance of three or four metres. Once he reached Place Dauphine he seemed to hesitate, then made towards the Brasserie Dauphine. He looked as if he was waiting for me. Seeing that I didn't approach him, he came towards me.

' "Since I'm going to have a drink, there's no reason why I shouldn't invite you to have one too."

'He looked as if he was making fun of me. He's a comedian, that man. I told him I never drank on duty, and he went in on his own. I saw him downing three or four brandies in a row, I don't know precisely.

'Then, after checking that I was still there and glancing at me again, he headed for Pont-Neuf. It was crowded at that time of day, and because the traffic was heavy, most of the drivers were honking their horns.

'We were approaching Quai de la Mégisserie, one behind the other, when I saw him hoist himself on to the parapet and jump into the Seine. It happened so quickly that only a few passers-by, the ones closest to him, were aware of it.

'I saw him emerge, less than three metres from a moored barge, and as the crowd grew denser, something almost comical happened. The boatman grabbed a long and heavy boat-hook and held out one end of it to Florentin, who seized the hook and allowed himself to be dragged from the water.

'A policeman came running and leaned over the undrowned man . . . I had been able to break away and get to the shore and then to the boat.

'There were onlookers everywhere, as if the event was important.

'I preferred not to get involved and to follow things from a distance. Just in case there happened to be a journalist around, I didn't want to tip them off . . . I don't know if I did the right thing.'

'You very much did the right thing. I can also tell you that Florentin wasn't putting himself at risk, because when we went swimming in the Allier he was the best swimmer of all of us. What happened next?'

'The kind boatman offered him a glass of rotgut, not suspecting that his drowned man had just gulped down three or four. Then the policeman took Florentin to the station in Les Halles.

'I didn't go in, for the reason I've already told you. They must have taken his name, his address, asked him a few questions. When he came out, he didn't see me, because I was having a sandwich in the bar opposite. He looked quite pitiful, with the old blanket that the police had lent him wrapped around his shoulders.

'He hailed a taxi and asked to be driven home. He changed his clothes. I could see him in the studio through the windows. He came out and noticed me. I was granted another glance, and a kind of grimace, and he walked to Place Blanche, where he went into a restaurant.

'He came out half an hour ago, after buying a newspaper, and when I left the cul-de-sac he was busy reading it, lying on his bed.'

Maigret had listened to this story with a certain bewilderment.

'Have you eaten?'

'I had a sandwich. I can see some here on the counter and I'm going to have a couple more. Torrence is due to take over from me at two in the morning.'

'Nice work,' Maigret sighed.

'Shall I call you if anything changes?'

'Any time you like.'

He nearly forgot his melon. Dusk was invading the apartment, and he went and stood eating by the window while Madame Maigret cleared the table.

It was clear that Florentin hadn't tried to commit suicide, because it was almost impossible for a good swimmer to drown in the Seine, in the middle of June, in front of hundreds of spectators. And a few metres from a barge!

Why had his former classmate jumped in the water? To make people think that the suspicions being heaped on him had left him in a state of despair?

'Is Lapointe well?'

Maigret smiled. He could see what his wife was getting at. She never asked him direct questions about his work, but sometimes she did throw him a line.

'He's very well. He has a few more hours on the beat in a courtyard off Boulevard Rochechouart.'

'Because of your school friend?'

'Yes. He's just given the passers-by on the Pont-Neuf a little show by suddenly throwing himself into the Seine.'

'You don't think he was trying to kill himself?'

'I'm sure of the opposite.'

What interest did Florentin have in drawing attention

to himself? Did he want his story to be told in the papers? It was unthinkable, and yet with him anything was possible.

'Shall we get some air?'

The streetlights on Boulevard Richard-Lenoir were lit, even though it wasn't yet completely dark. They weren't the only ones walking along the pavement, peacefully, with no other aim than to taste the cool air after a hot day. They went to bed at eleven. The next morning the sun was in its place, and the air was already warm. A faint smell of tar was beginning to rise from the street, the smell of summer when the bitumen begins to soften.

Once he got to his office, Maigret had to deal with a large amount of mail, then attend the morning briefing. The papers mentioned the crime on Rue Notre-Dame-de-Lorette without many details, and he gave a brief summary of what he knew.

'He didn't confess?'

'No.'

'Do you have evidence against him?'

'Some presumptions.'

He saw little point in adding that Florentin was an old schoolmate. When he got back to his office, he made a point of calling Janvier.

'In fact, Joséphine Papet had four regular visitors. Two of them, François Paré and the man called Courcel, have been identified, and I will look into them this morning. You take care of the two others. Question the neighbours, the local shopkeepers, question whoever you like, but bring me their names and addresses.'

Janvier couldn't help smiling, because Maigret himself was aware that the task was almost impossible.

'I'm counting on you.'

'Yes, chief.'

After which, Maigret called the pathologist. Sadly, it was no longer good old Dr Paul, who, when he dined in town, took a malicious pleasure in going into great detail about his autopsies.

'Have you found the bullet, doctor?'

The pathologist had started by reading him the report that he was busy writing.

Joséphine Papet was a healthy woman, in the prime of life. All of her organs were in a good state, and she took great care with her appearance.

As to the gunshot, it had been fired from less than a metre but more than fifty centimetres away.

'The bullet lodged at the base of the skull following a slightly rising trajectory . . .'

Maigret couldn't help thinking of Florentin's tall physique. Did that mean that he was sitting down when he fired the gun?

He asked the question.

'Could someone sitting down . . .'

'No. I'm not talking about an angle like that. I said slightly rising. I've sent the bullet to Gastinne-Renette for a specialist report. In my view, it wasn't fired with an automatic, but with a barrel revolver of quite an old model.'

'Was death instantaneous?'

'Twenty to thirty seconds, in my view.'

'So that no one could have saved her?'

'Certainly not.'

'Thank you, doctor.'

Torrence had come back to the office. A new officer called Dieudonné had gone to take over from him.

'What's he doing?'

'He got up at seven thirty, shaved and, after washing perfunctorily, went in his slippers to have two coffees and some croissants at the bar on the corner. Then he went into the telephone cabin. He seemed to hesitate and came back out without using the phone.

'Several times he turned round to look at me. I don't know what he's usually like, but he struck me as weary and discouraged.

'At the kiosk on Place Blanche he bought the papers and looked through two or three of them, standing on the pavement.

'In the end he went back home. Dieudonné arrived. I gave him his instructions and came to give you my report.'

'Did he talk to anybody?'

'No . . . Or rather he did, but you could hardly call it talking. While he was going to buy the papers, the painter from next door arrived. I don't know where he sleeps, but it certainly isn't in his studio. Florentin said to him:

' "How are you?"

'And the other man repeated exactly the same words, after which he studied me curiously. He must be wondering what we're doing in the courtyard, one after the other. He showed the same curiosity when Dieudonné took my place.'

Maigret took his hat off the hook and went to the

courtyard. He could have brought an inspector with him and taken one of the black cars lined up along the buildings.

He preferred to go on foot, to cross Pont Saint-Michel and head towards Boulevard Saint-Germain. He had never had the opportunity to step inside the Ministry of Public Works and he hesitated between the different staircases, each of which bore a different letter.

'Are you looking for something?'

'Navigable Waterways.'

'Staircase C, right at the top.'

He saw no lift. The staircase was the same shade of grey as the one at Quai des Orfèvres. On each floor, black arrows were painted on the walls, with the names of the various offices to which the corridors led.

When he was on the third floor he found the right arrow and pushed open a door bearing the words: 'Come in without knocking'.

Four male and two female clerks were working in the office, separated from the visitors by a balustrade. On the walls were yellowed maps, like the ones at the lycée in Moulins in the old days.

'Can I help you?'

'I'd like to speak to Monsieur Paré, please.'

'Who shall I say it is?'

He hesitated. Not wishing to compromise the head of department, who might have been a decent man, he didn't hand over his card.

'My name is Maigret.'

The young clerk frowned, looked at him with greater attention and finally walked away shrugging his shoulders.

He was only gone for a few moments, and when he came back he opened a gate.

'Monsieur Paré will see you immediately.'

He opened a door, and Maigret found himself facing a middle-aged man, stout and very dignified, standing up, who pointed him to a chair, not without a certain solemnity.

'I've been waiting for you, Monsieur Maigret.'

The morning newspaper was on his desk. He sat down in turn, slowly, as if it was a ritual gesture, and rested his arms on the sides of his armchair.

'I don't need to tell you that I am in a very unpleasant situation.'

He wasn't smiling. He didn't look as if he smiled often. He was a calm and level-headed man who weighed each of his words.

3.

The office could have been Maigret's before the premises of the Police Judiciaire were modernized, and on the mantelpiece the inspector found the same black marble clock which he had in front of his eyes all day, and which he had never managed to set correctly.

As to the man, he was the image of the clock. His attitude was plainly that of the senior civil servant who was both cautious and self-assured, and who must have been deeply humiliated suddenly finding himself in the hot seat.

His features were soft. His thinning brown hair was combed over a bald patch that it only partially concealed, and he had a small moustache so black that it must have been dyed. The white skin of his hands was covered with long hairs.

'I am grateful to you, Monsieur Maigret, for not summoning me to the Police Judiciaire, and for troubling yourself to come in person.'

'I'm trying to give this event the minimum of publicity.'

'Indeed, there are hardly any details in this morning's papers.'

'Had you known Joséphine Papet for long?'

'About three years. I'm sorry if the name made me start, but I always called her Josée. I didn't find out her real name for several months.'

'I understand. How did you meet her?'

'In the most ordinary way . . . I'm fifty-five, inspector. So I was fifty-two at the time, and you will have trouble believing me if I tell you that I have never cheated on my wife.

'And yet about ten years ago she fell ill, and our relationship has not been easy, because she suffers from nervous exhaustion.'

'Do you have children?'

'Three daughters. The oldest is married to a shipowner in La Rochelle. The second teaches at a school in Tunis, and the third, also married, lives in Paris, in the sixteenth arrondissement. I have five grandchildren in all, the oldest of whom is about to turn twelve. We have lived in the same building, in Versailles, for thirty years. You can see that for a long time I have lived an untroubled life, the ordinary life of a scrupulous civil servant.'

He spoke slowly, choosing his words carefully, a prudent man. There was no trace of humour in what he said, or in the expression on his face. Did he ever burst out laughing? It was unlikely. And if he ever smiled, it must have been a lifeless kind of smile.

'You asked me where I met her. Sometimes, after work, I stop for a moment in a brasserie on the corner of Boulevard Saint-Germain and Rue de Solférino. That was what happened that day. It was raining, and I still remember the water trickling down the windows.

'I sat down in my usual place, and the waiter, who has known me for years, brought me my glass of port.

'At the next table a young woman was busy writing a

letter and having problems with the bar's fountain pen. The violet ink in the inkwell had started to dry out.

'She was a respectable person, modestly dressed in a well-cut navy-blue suit.

' "Waiter, is this the only pen you have?"

' "Unfortunately it's the only one we have. These days all the customers have their own ballpoint pens."

'Without any ulterior motive, I took mine out of my pocket and held it out to her.

' "If you'll allow me . . ."

'She looked at me and smiled gratefully. That's how things started. She didn't write for long. She drank some tea.

' "Do you come here often?" she asked me, returning my pen.

' "Almost every day."

' "I love the atmosphere of these old brasseries, with all their regular customers."

' "Do you live locally?"

' "No. I live on Rue Notre-Dame-de-Lorette, but I come to the Left Bank quite often." '

His innocence was there to be seen in his expression.

'You see how fortuitous our meeting was. She didn't come the next day. The day after that, I found her in the same place, and she gave me a faint smile.

'She seemed gentle and calm, with something reassuring about her demeanour and her facial expressions.

'We exchanged a few words. I told her I lived in Versailles, and I think that from that day onwards I talked to her about my wife and daughters . . . She saw me getting into my car.

'I may surprise you by telling you that it went on like that for over a month, and that on the days when I didn't find her in the brasserie I felt frustrated.

'In my eyes she was just a friend, and I had nothing else in mind. With my wife I have to watch my words, to risk being misunderstood and causing a fit of hysterics.

'In the days when my daughters lived with us, the apartment was noisy and full of life, my wife was still active and cheerful. You can't imagine how it feels to go back to an apartment that's too big, too empty, where all that awaits you are anxious, suspicious eyes.'

Maigret was lighting his pipe and held out his tobacco pouch.

'Thank you. I haven't smoked for a long time . . . Don't imagine that I'm trying to excuse my conduct.

'Every Wednesday I used to go to a meeting of a charitable association of which I'm a member. One Wednesday I didn't go, and Mademoiselle Papet took me to her place . . .

'I learned that she lived on her own, on a very modest allowance left to her by her parents, and that she'd tried in vain to find work.'

'She didn't talk to you about her family?'

'Her father, who was an officer, was killed in the war when she was only a child, and she was brought up by her mother in the provinces. She had a brother.'

'Did you see him?'

'Only once. He's an engineer and travels a lot. One Wednesday when I turned up early I found him in the apartment, and she took advantage of the fact to introduce us.

'A distinguished fellow, intelligent, much older than her. He developed a new method of eliminating toxins from car exhaust fumes.'

'Is he tall, thin, with an agile face and pale eyes?'

François Paré looked surprised.

'Do you know him?'

'I have met him, yes. Tell me, did you give Josée a lot of money?'

The civil servant blushed and looked away.

'I enjoy a certain degree of affluence, and perhaps even a little more than that. A brother of my mother's left me two farms in Normandy, and I could have retired years ago. But what would I have done with my days?'

'Could it be said that you kept her?'

'Not exactly. I enabled her not to worry about minor expenses, to surround herself with a little more comfort.'

'You saw her only on Wednesdays?'

'It's the only day of the week that I have an excuse to stay in Paris for the night. The older my wife and I get, the more jealous she becomes.'

'It's never occurred to her to follow you when you leave the ministry?'

'No. She barely leaves the apartment. She has grown so thin that she can hardly stand up, and one doctor after another has given up on healing her . . .'

'Did Mademoiselle Papet claim that you were her only lover?'

'At first, that was a word that we never uttered. It's accurate in a sense, because I won't conceal the fact that we had intimate relations.

'But there was a different bond between us. We were both lonely people, doing our best in the face of fate. I don't know if you understand. We could talk openly to one another. She was my friend, and I was her friend.'

'Were you jealous?'

He started and gave Maigret a harsh look, as if he resented the question.

'I've told you that all my life I've never had affairs. I told you how old I am. I haven't hidden from you the importance that this trusting friendship had assumed in my eyes. I waited impatiently for Wednesdays. I lived for Wednesday evening. It enabled me to bear everything.'

'So you would have been devastated if you had learned that she had another lover?'

'Certainly. That would have been the end.'

'The end of what?'

'Of everything. Of the small happiness granted to me for three years.'

'You only met the brother once?'

'Yes.'

'You had no suspicions?'

'What would I have suspected?'

'You didn't find anyone else in the apartment?'

He smiled faintly.

'Once, a few weeks ago. When I was coming out of the lift, quite a young man was leaving the apartment.'

'A red-haired man?'

He was stunned.

'How did you know? In that case, you will also be aware that he's an insurance agent. I confess that I followed him and saw him going into a bar on Rue Fontaine, where they seemed to know him.

'When I questioned Josée, she wasn't embarrassed in the slightest.

' "It's the third time he's tried to get me to sign up for a life insurance policy," she explained. "On whose behalf would I take out life insurance? I must have his card somewhere . . ."

'She looked in her drawers and actually found a visiting card in the name of Jean-Luc Bodard, a sales representative with Continentale, on Avenue de l'Opéra. It isn't a big company, but it has an excellent reputation. I called the head of personnel, who confirmed to me that Jean-Luc Bodard was one of their agents.'

Maigret was smoking slowly, taking little puffs, trying to gain some time, because there was nothing pleasant about the task ahead of him.

'Did you go to Rue Notre-Dame-de-Lorette yesterday?'

'I was detained by the minister's private secretary. I rang the bell and was surprised that no one came and opened the door. I rang again, knocked, but there was no answer.'

'You weren't curious enough to ask the concierge?'

'I'm scared of that woman and have as little to do with her as possible. I didn't go home immediately. I dined on my own, in a restaurant at Porte de Versailles, because I was supposed to attend the charity meeting.'

'When did you find out what had happened?'

'This morning, when I was shaving. They mentioned it on the radio without going into details. It wasn't till I got here that I read the paper . . . I'm crushed . . . I don't understand . . .'

'You didn't happen to go there yesterday, between three and four?'

The man's mood turned bitter.

'I understand what you're getting at. I didn't leave the office in the afternoon and my colleagues will be able to confirm that. But I would rather my name wasn't mentioned.'

Poor man! He was worried, anxious, overwhelmed. Everything he had clung to lately was crumbling, and he was struggling to preserve his dignity.

'I thought that the concierge, or the brother, if he is in Paris, might talk to you about me.'

'There is no brother, Monsieur Paré.'

The man frowned in disbelief, ready to lose his temper.

'I'm sorry to disappoint you, but I have to tell you the truth. The person introduced to you under the name of Léon Papet is really called Léon Florentin, and as chance would have it we were fellow pupils at the lycée in Moulins . . .'

'I don't understand.'

'As soon as you left Joséphine Papet he entered the apartment. He had a key. Did you ever have one?'

'No. I never asked for one . . . It would never have occurred to me . . .'

'He regularly stayed in the apartment and only disappeared when visitors were expected.'

'You said visitors? In the plural?'

Very pale, he remained rigid in his armchair.

'There were four of you, not counting Florentin.'

'You mean . . .?'

'That Joséphine Papet was kept by four different lovers. One of them preceded you by several years, and a very long while ago they lived together in the apartment.'

'Have you seen him?'

'Not yet.'

'Who is he?'

Deep down, François Paré was still sceptical.

'A certain Fernand Courcel, who runs a ball-bearings company with his brother. The factory is in Rouen, the Paris offices are on Boulevard Voltaire. He's about your age, and quite fat.'

'I can hardly believe it.'

'His day is Thursday, and he's the only one who spends the night in the apartment.'

'I don't suppose this is a trap?'

'What do you mean?'

'I don't know. They say the police sometimes use unexpected methods. This whole business seems so unlikely to me.'

'There's another one, the Saturday man. I have little information about him, but I know he walks with a limp.'

'And the fourth one?'

The man struggled to maintain his composure; but his hands, covered with their long hairs, were clenched so tightly on the arm of the chair that the knuckles were pale.

'He's the redhead, the insurance salesman you met one day by chance.'

'He really is an insurance salesman. I checked myself.'

'You can be an insurance salesman and the lover of a pretty woman at the same time.'

'I don't understand anything any more . . . You didn't know her, or you'd be as incredulous as me. I've never met such a wise, simple, calm woman. I have three daughters, and they've taught me about women . . . I would have trusted Josée more than any of my children.'

'I'm sorry to have had to open your eyes.'

'I assume you're sure about everything you've just told me?'

'If you like, I'll have Florentin repeat it to you.'

'I have absolutely no desire to meet this individual, or any of the three others. If I understand correctly, this fellow Florentin was what you might call her live-in lover?'

'More or less. He's tried a bit of all sorts of things in his life. He's failed at all of them. But he still exerts a certain charm on women.'

'He's almost my age.'

'Give or take a couple of years, but yes . . . His advantage over you is that he's available day and night. And he doesn't take anything seriously. To him, every day is a blank page that you fill up as you see fit, according to your mood.'

Paré, however, had a conscience, problems, regrets. His face, his whole demeanour expressed everything to do with the serious side of life.

One might almost have imagined that he carried his office with him, if not the whole ministry, and Maigret had difficulty imagining his tête-à-têtes with Josée.

It was a good thing that she was placid. She must have been able to listen with a smile, for hours on end, to the confidences of a man worn down by fate and misfortunes.

All of a sudden, Maigret started forming a more precise idea of her. She had a strong practical sense, and was good at doing calculations. She had bought herself a house in Montmartre, and she had forty-eight thousand francs stowed away. Wouldn't a second house have followed, and then a third?

Some women count in houses, as if stone were the only solid thing in the world.

'You weren't expecting any drama, then, Monsieur Paré?'

'The prospect never occurred to me for a single second. There was nothing more reassuring than her, her life, her apartment . . .'

'Did she tell you where she came from originally?'

'Poitiers, if I remember correctly.'

Out of prudence, she must have given each of them a different place of birth.

'Did she seem educated?'

'She graduated from secondary school before spending time as secretary to a lawyer.'

'Do you know his name?'

'I paid it no attention.'

'She never married?'

'Not to my knowledge.'

'You weren't surprised by the books she read?'

'She was sentimental, essentially quite naive, and that's

64

why she preferred pulp novels. She was the first to laugh at that little flaw.'

'I won't trouble you more than is absolutely necessary. I only ask you to think, to search through your memories. An apparently insignificant phrase or detail might help us.'

François Paré got to his feet, tall and heavy, and paused before extending a hand.

'For now, nothing comes to mind.'

Then, hesitantly, and in a fainter voice:

'Do you know if she suffered a great deal?'

'According to the pathologist, death was instantaneous.'

His lips moved. He was probably praying.

'Thank you for showing so much tact. I'm only sorry that we didn't meet under different circumstances.'

'Me too, Monsieur Paré.'

Ouf! Maigret exhaled noisily as soon as he was on the stairs. He felt as if he had just emerged from a tunnel, back in the open air, in the real world.

Certainly, he had learned nothing precise, nothing immediately usable, but his interview with the head of Navigable Waterways had brought the image of the young woman to life.

Was the letter written in a brasserie with a middle-class clientele her usual tactic, or had that only been a matter of chance?

The first of her known lovers, Fernand Courcel, seemed to have met her when she was twenty-five. What had she been doing in those days? He couldn't imagine her, with her modest appearance, walking the pavements near the Madeleine or the Champs-Élysées.

Was she really a secretary to somebody, lawyer or not?

A light breeze stirred the leaves of the trees on Boulevard Saint-Germain, and Maigret looked as if he was going for a stroll, breathing in the morning air. On a little street that led him towards the river embankments, he passed by an old-fashioned bistro where a lorry was unloading barrels of wine.

He stepped inside and leaned on the bar.

'What sort of wine is it?'

'Sancerre. It's where I'm from, and I bring it in from my brother-in-law's.'

It was both dry and fruity. The counter was a real zinc counter, and there was sawdust on the red tiles.

'Same again, please.'

What a strange job he had! He still had three men to see, three of the lovers of Joséphine, who seemed to have been a seller of dreams.

François Paré would have difficulty finding anyone else to pour his old heart out to. Florentin was reduced to his studio in Montmartre and a mattress on the floor in a windowless room.

'Onwards,' he sighed, leaving the bistro and heading for the Police Judiciaire.

Another creature doomed to be disappointed, to be stripped of his illusions.

When Maigret reached the top of the stairs, and then the long corridor of the Police Judiciaire, he glanced instinctively at the glazed waiting room that the inspectors facetiously called 'the aquarium'.

He was quite surprised to see Léon Florentin, sitting on one of the uncomfortable green velvet chairs next to a stranger. This man was quite small and fat and had a round face and blue eyes; under ordinary circumstances he must have enjoyed the good life.

Right now, however, while Florentin talked to him in a low voice, he clutched a rolled-up handkerchief in his hand and dabbed his eyes every now and again.

In front of them, Inspector Dieudonné indifferently scanned the racing pages of a newspaper.

Neither of them spotted him, and, once he was in his office, Maigret rang his bell. Old Joseph half-opened the door almost immediately.

'Is there someone to see me?'

'Two people, inspector.'

'Who came first?'

'That one.'

He showed him Florentin's card.

'And the other one?'

'He turned up about ten minutes ago and seemed very emotional.'

It was Fernand Courcel, of Courcel Brothers, ball-bearings, in Rouen. The card also bore the address of the offices on Boulevard Voltaire.

'Who shall I show in first?'

'Bring me Monsieur Courcel.'

He sat down at his desk and glanced through the open window at the shimmering air outside.

'Please come in. Do take a seat.'

The man was very small and very fat but appeared to

be in good health. He gave off a pleasing vitality, an unfeigned cordiality.

'You don't know me, inspector . . .'

'If you hadn't come this morning, I would have gone to your office, Monsieur Courcel.'

The man's blue eyes looked at him with surprise, but without fear.

'So you know?'

'I know that you were a great friend of Mademoiselle Papet, and that you must have had a shock this morning when you listened to the radio and read the paper.'

Courcel's lips quivered as if he was about to burst into tears, but he managed to restrain himself.

'Please forgive me . . . I'm upset . . . I was more than a friend to her . . .'

'I know.'

'In that case I haven't got much else to tell you, because I haven't the slightest idea what could have happened . . . She was the sweetest, most discreet woman . . .'

'Do you know the man who was with you in the waiting room?'

The factory-owner, who seemed so little like a ball-bearings manufacturer, looked at him with surprise.

'You didn't know she had a brother?'

'Did you first meet him a long time ago?'

'About three years ago. More or less at the time when he came back from Uruguay.'

'Did he live there for a long time?'

'You haven't questioned him?'

'I'm curious to learn what he told you.'

'He's an architect and was employed by the Uruguayan government to draw up the plans for a new town.'

'Was he at Joséphine Papet's?'

'He was.'

'Did you turn up early, or on the spur of the moment?'

'I confess that I can't remember.'

The question shocked him, and he frowned, furrowing his very blond eyebrows. His hair was blond too, almost white, like the hair that some babies have, and his skin was a tender pink.

'I don't see what you're trying to get at.'

'Did you see him again?'

'Three or four times . . .'

'Always at Rue Notre-Dame-de-Lorette?'

'No . . . He came to my office to talk to me about a plan for a modern beach resort, with hotels, villas and bungalows, between Le Grau-du-Roi and Palavas.'

'And he wanted to get you involved?'

'Exactly. I admit that his project was a good one, and that it will probably turn into something. Unfortunately, I can't withdraw any money from our company, which belongs to my brother as much as it does to me.'

'You didn't give him anything?'

He blushed. He was startled by Maigret's attitude.

'I gave him a few thousand francs to print up the plans.'

'Was it printed? Were you given a copy?'

'I told you I wasn't interested.'

'And did he scrounge off you again after that?'

'Last year, although I don't like the word. Pioneers always encounter obstacles. His office in Montpellier—'

'He lives in Montpellier?'

'You didn't know?'

They were talking at cross-purposes, and Fernand Courcel was growing impatient.

'Why don't you call him and ask him these questions?'

'It will be his turn in due course.'

'You seem ill disposed towards him.'

'Not at all, Monsieur Courcel. I will even confess that he's an old schoolmate.'

The little man had taken a cigarette from a gold case.

'May I?'

'Please do. How many times did you give him money?'

He had to think.

'Three times. The last time, he had left his chequebook in Montpellier.'

'What was he talking to you about, a few minutes ago, in the waiting room?'

'Do I have to give you an answer?'

'It would be better.'

'It's such an awkward subject . . . Well!'

He sighed, stretched his little legs and blew out the smoke from his cigarette.

'He doesn't know anything about what his sister did with her money. And neither did I, because it has nothing to do with me. At the moment he's short of money, he's invested everything in his project, and he's asked me to contribute to the costs of the funeral.'

Courcel was outraged to see Maigret smiling broadly. It was really too much!

'Forgive me. You will understand. First of all, you should be aware that the one you know by the name of Léon Papet is really called Léon Florentin. He's the son of a pastry-chef in Moulins, and we went to the Lycée Banville together.'

'He's not the brother of . . .'

'No, my dear sir. He's not her brother, or her cousin, which doesn't stop him living with her.'

'You mean . . .'

He had got to his feet, unable to stay in his chair.

'No!' he exclaimed. 'It's impossible, Josée couldn't possibly have . . .'

He paced back and forth, spilling the ash from his cigarette on the carpet.

'Don't forget, inspector, that I've known her for ten years. I lived with her, at first, before I was married. I was the one who found her the apartment on Rue Notre-Dame-de-Lorette and decorated it in accordance with her tastes.'

'She was twenty-five?'

'Yes. I was thirty-two. My father was still alive, and I wasn't very involved with our company, because my brother Gaston ran the Paris office.'

'Where and how did you meet her?'

'I was expecting that question, and I know what you're going to think. I got to know her in Montmartre, in a nightclub that no longer exists, called the Nouvel Adam.'

'Did she perform there?'

'No. She was a "hostess". That doesn't mean that she went to bed with every customer who asked her to. I found her alone at a table, melancholy and wearing hardly any make-up, in a simple black dress. She was so shy that I was reluctant to speak to her.'

'Did you spend the evening with her?'

'Of course. She told me about her childhood.'

'Where did she tell you she came from?'

'From La Rochelle. Her father, who was a fisherman, died in a shipwreck and she has four younger brothers and sisters.'

'What about her mother? I'm guessing she's dead.'

Courcel gave him a furious look.

'If you want me to go on . . .'

'I'm sorry. You see, none of that exists.'

'She hasn't got four brothers and sisters?'

'No. And she didn't need to work in a cabaret in Montmartre to help to bring them up. Because that's what she told you, isn't it?'

Courcel sat down again, hesitantly, head lowered.

'I find it hard to believe you. I loved her passionately.'

'And yet you got married?'

'I married one of my cousins, it's true. I felt I was getting older. I wanted to have children.'

'You live in Rouen?'

'For most of the week.'

'But not Thursdays.'

'How do you know that?'

'On Thursdays you went for dinner with Josée and then, after going to the cinema or the theatre, you went back to spend the night in Rue Notre-Dame-de-Lorette.'

'That's right. I wanted to split up with her but I couldn't do it.'

'Does your wife know?'

'No, of course not.'

'Your brother?'

'I had to let Gaston in on it, because I'm supposed to be visiting our office in Marseille.'

The little man added with a certain candour:

'He treats me like an idiot.'

Maigret managed not to smile.

'When I think that even just now I was ready to weep in front of that man who . . .'

'Florentin isn't the only one.'

'What are you insinuating?'

'If she had died in some other way I would have left you in your ignorance, Monsieur Courcel. But she was murdered. My task is to find the person who killed her, and that can only happen in a climate of truth.'

'Do you know who fired the gun?'

'Not yet. There were four of you, apart from Florentin, who regularly paid her visits.'

He shook his head as if he still couldn't believe it.

'At one point I was tempted to marry her. If it weren't for Gaston, it's likely that . . .'

'Wednesday was the day of a senior civil servant who didn't spend the night in the apartment.'

'Have you met him?'

'This morning.'

'Did he confess?'

'He didn't hide his secrets from me, or their nature.'

'How old is he?'

'Fifty-five. Have you ever met a man with a limp, either in the lift or in the apartment?'

'No.'

'Because there was a man with a limp as well, a middle-aged man whom I will soon track down if my inspectors haven't done so already.'

'And then?' sighed the man, in a hurry to get it all over with.

'And then a redhead, younger than the rest of you. He's only about thirty, and works for an insurance company.'

'I don't imagine you knew her when she was alive?'

'That's right.'

'If you had known her, you would understand my dismay. You would have sworn that she was frankness personified. A frankness so intense that it spilled over into naivety.'

'Did you give her something to live on?'

'I had to press her to accept it. She wanted to work in a shop, a lingerie boutique, for example. And yet she didn't have a robust constitution. She sometimes had dizzy spells. She always thought I was giving her too much money.'

An idea came to him at last, one that he hadn't imagined until then.

'And the others? Did they also . . .?'

'I fear so, Monsieur Courcel. Each of you kept her, except perhaps the redhead, as I shall shortly find out. It's true, in any case, of the civil servant I met this morning . . .'

'So what did she do with the money? Her tastes were so simple.'

'She began by buying herself a house on Rue du Mont-Cenis. And when she died they found forty-eight thousand francs in her apartment. Now, try to overcome your distress and think. I won't ask you where you were yesterday between three and four in the afternoon.'

'I was in my car, on the way back from Rouen, and I must have been passing through the Saint-Cloud tunnel at about a quarter past three.'

He stopped short and looked at Maigret with amazement.

'Does that mean that you suspect me?'

'I don't suspect anyone, and my question is purely a matter of routine . . . At what time did you get to your office?'

'I didn't go there straight away. I stopped for a while in a bar on Rue de Ponthieu where I usually bet on the horses. In fact, I got to Boulevard Voltaire at about five fifteen. On paper I'm my brother's business partner. I go to the factory twice a week. I have an office and a secretary on Boulevard Voltaire, but the firm would get along just as well without me.'

'Isn't your brother angry with you?'

'On the contrary. The less I do, the more satisfied he is, because that way he feels that he's the only boss.'

'What make is your car, Monsieur Courcel?'

'Jaguar. A convertible. I've always had convertibles. Pale-blue bodywork. You want the registration?'

'There's no need.'

'When I think that not only Josée but her so-called brother . . . What did you say his name was?'

'Florentin. His father made the best cakes in Moulins.'

Courcel clenched his little fists.

'Calm down. Unless there are any unexpected developments, your name will not be published, and all of this will remain confidential. Is your wife jealous?'

'Probably, but not in a particularly fierce way. She suspects me of having affairs from time to time, in Marseille or Paris.'

'And do you, apart from Josée?'

'It happens. I'm curious, like all men.'

He looked for his hat, which he had left in the waiting room. Maigret went with him, worried that he would pick a fight with Florentin.

Florentin looked at both of them lugubriously as if to discover whether Courcel had taken the bait.

When the factory-owner had disappeared, Inspector Dieudonné, who had got up when Maigret came in, asked:

'Shall I give you my report?'

'Has something happened?'

'No. After having breakfast at the bistro on the corner he went home and didn't take the Métro to come here until nine thirty. He asked to see you. The other person arrived, and they shook hands. I didn't hear what they said to each other.'

'That's enough for today.'

Maigret gestured to Florentin.

'Come here.'

He brought him into his office and, once the door was

closed, he looked at him for a long time. Florentin kept his head low, and his big bony body seemed softer, as if it were about to cave in.

'You're even more of a crook than I thought.'

'I know.'

'Why did you do it?'

'I didn't know I was going to meet him.'

'What did you come to do here?'

He raised his head and gave Maigret a pitiful look.

'How much money do you think I've got left in my wallet?'

'It doesn't matter.'

'On the contrary, it does matter. I've got exactly one fifty-centime coin left. And there isn't a shop, a bistro or a restaurant in the district that would give me credit.'

It was Maigret's turn to be bewildered, almost as much as the chubby man had been a little earlier.

'Did you come to ask me for money?'

'Who else would you expect me to ask, in my position? I suppose you told that idiotic stuffed shirt Paré that I'm not Josée's brother.'

'Obviously.'

'It must have been quite a shock, being disillusioned like that.'

'In any case, he has a serious alibi . . . He was in his office yesterday, between three and four.'

'When I saw that suckling pig coming into the waiting room, I told myself I still had a hope.'

'The price of the funeral! Aren't you ashamed of yourself?'

Florentin shrugged.

'Well, you know, it's out of shame that . . . Bear in mind that I suspected he would talk to you. Since I got here first, I still hoped that you would see me before him.'

He fell silent, while Maigret went and stood by the window. The air from outside had seldom seemed so pure.

'What are they going to do with the forty-eight thousand francs?'

The inspector gave a start. Wasn't it incredible that Florentin should have thought of that money at just that moment?

'Don't you realize that I have no means of earning a living? The antiques bring in the odd banknote from time to time. I'll be straight with you. It was a façade.'

'I'd worked that out.'

'So while I'm waiting to sort myself out . . .'

'What do you think you'll do?'

'If need be, I'll unload vegetables at les Halles.'

'I should warn you that you're forbidden to leave Paris.'

'I'm still a suspect?'

'Until the murderer is behind bars. Do you really know nothing about the man with a limp?'

'Josée only knew him by his first name, Victor. He never talked to her about his wife, or his children. She didn't know what he did for a living, but he gave the impression of being well off. His clothes were well cut, his shirts made to measure. One detail comes back to me. Once, taking out his wallet, he dropped a season ticket for the Paris– Bordeaux line.'

That was a place for the inspectors to start. There

couldn't be that many season tickets on the Paris–Bordeaux line.

'You see. I'm doing my best to cooperate.'

Maigret understood, and he too pulled his wallet from his pocket and took out a hundred-franc note.

'Try and make it last a while.'

'Are you still going to have me followed?'

'Yes.'

He opened the door to the inspectors' room a crack.

'Leroy.'

He gave him instructions and couldn't avoid the hand that his old schoolmate extended to him.

4.

It was three o'clock, and Maigret was standing by the open window, pipe in his mouth, hands in his pockets, in a familiar pose.

The sun was shining, the sky was a solid blue, there wasn't a cloud, and yet long drops of rain had started falling diagonally, a long distance apart, splattering on the ground and leaving broad black marks.

'Come in, Lucas,' he said without turning round, when the door half opened.

He had sent him up to the attics of the Palais de Justice to check in Records and find out whether Florentin had a criminal file.

'Three convictions, chief, nothing really serious.'

'Fraud?'

'The first, twenty-two years ago, for a bad cheque. He was living in a furnished apartment on the Avenue de Wagram and had rented offices on the Champs-Élysées. It was something to do with importing exotic fruits. Six months suspended.

'Eight years later he was sentenced to a year for fraud and using counterfeit money. His address was in Montparnasse, in a small hotel. It wasn't suspended. So he's done time.

'Bad cheque again five years ago. No fixed abode . . .'

'Thank you.'

'Anything else for me?'

'Go to Rue Notre-Dame-de-Lorette to question the shopkeepers. Janvier's done it already, but not with the same goal. I'd like to know whether yesterday, between three and four, anyone saw a sky-blue Jaguar convertible parked in the street or somewhere nearby. Question the mechanics too.'

He was left alone, frowning. Moers' specialists had had hardly any success. Joséphine Papet's prints all over the apartment, as might have been expected.

And yet there were none on the door handles; they had all been carefully wiped.

There were prints from Florentin, including some in the wardrobe and the bathroom, but nothing on the bedside table drawer, from which the murderer must in all likelihood have taken the revolver.

Maigret had been struck, entering the apartment for the first time, by how clean it was. Joséphine Papet did not employ a maid or a housekeeper. He imagined her, all morning, tidying the rooms with a headscarf covering her hair, while the radio played faintly.

He was wearing his grumpy face, as he did when he wasn't contented with himself, and indeed he did have concerns.

If Florentin hadn't been his fellow pupil in Moulins, wouldn't he already have instructed the examining magistrate to issue a warrant against him?

The pastry-chef's son had never been what one calls a friend. Even at school, young Maigret had had mixed feelings about him.

Florentin was funny and made the class laugh and was willing to risk punishment to amuse his classmates.

But hadn't there been something like defiance, even aggression, in his attitude?

He mocked everyone, giving comic imitations of the teachers' tics and expressions.

His retorts were funny. He gauged their effect on the faces of his audience and he would have been put out if the laughter hadn't come.

Wasn't he already on the margins? Didn't he feel different? And wasn't that why his humour so often had an edge to it?

In Paris, as an adult, he hadn't changed, as he went through ups and downs and dark times, including prison.

He refused to be beaten, he was still a handsome man, with a natural elegance even in a threadbare suit.

He lied without noticing. He had always lied and he wasn't embarrassed when his interlocutor noticed. He seemed to be saying:

'That was plausible, though! Shame it didn't work.'

He must have frequented Fouquet's, other bars on the Champs-Élysées and the surrounding area, the cabarets, all the places where people go to forget their troubles.

Basically Maigret suspected that he was an anxious person. Playing the comedian was only a façade to defend himself against a pitiful truth.

He was a failure, a stereotypical failure, and more seriously, more painfully, he was an ageing failure.

Was it out of pity that Maigret hadn't arrested him? Or because Florentin had accumulated too much evidence against him, even though he was intelligent?

Taking Josée's savings away, for example, and wrapping the biscuit tin in that morning's newspaper. Couldn't he have found a hiding place other than his hovel on Boulevard Rochechouart, which the police were bound to search?

The quarter of an hour that he had spent waiting in the wardrobe after the shot was fired . . .

Was he afraid to find himself face to face with the murderer?

Choosing Maigret, while it would have been so easy to alert the local chief inspector . . .

Maigret had every reason to arrest him. For a few weeks there had also been the visits from the redhead, a young man, perhaps likely to take his place, and thus steal his livelihood.

Janvier knocked, came in without waiting and slumped on a chair.

'We've got him at last, chief.'

'The limping man?'

'Yes. I can't remember how many phone calls I've made, including a good half dozen to Bordeaux. When I spoke to the railways, I almost had to go down on my knees to get them to look among their season-ticket holders straight away.'

He lit a cigarette and stretched his legs.

'Now I hope that my limping man is the right one. I don't know if I've done the right thing, but I've asked him to call in and see you. He'll be here in a quarter of an hour . . .'

'I would rather have met him at his home.'

'He lives in Bordeaux. In Paris, he has an apartment at the Hôtel Scribe, a stone's throw from his offices on Rue Auber.'

'Who is he?'

'If my information is correct, in Bordeaux he's an important figure in the Chartrons, the district where all the old families have grand homes on the waterfront. He is a wine dealer, of course, working mostly with Germany and the Scandinavian countries.'

'Have you seen him?'

'I called him.'

'Did he seem surprised?'

'At first he became very arrogant and asked me if it was a joke. When I assured him that I was really from the Police Judiciaire and you wanted to see him, he declared that he had nothing to do with the police, and that they should leave him in peace if they knew what was good for them. I told him about the Rue Notre-Dame-de-Lorette.'

'Did he react?'

'There was a silence, then he muttered:

'"When does Detective Inspector Maigret want to see me?"

'"As soon as possible."

'"When I've finished going through my mail, I'll call in at Quai des Orfèvres."'

Janvier added:

'His name is Lamotte, Victor Lamotte. If you like, while you are seeing him, I'll call the Police Judiciaire in Bordeaux for some additional information.'

'Good idea.'

'You don't seem happy.'

Maigret shrugged. Wasn't it always like this at a certain point in an inquiry, when nothing precise was known? The previous day he hadn't known these people, apart from Florentin.

That morning, he had received a podgy little man who had seemed quite dreary. If Courcel hadn't had the good luck to be the son of a ball-bearing manufacturer, what would he have been? Travelling salesman? Or another Florentin, half parasite, half crook?

Joseph came and announced his visitor and walked ahead of him. The man did in fact walk with a limp. Maigret was surprised by his white hair, by the softness of his face, and guessed that he was about sixty.

'Come in, Monsieur Lamotte. I'm sorry for bothering you. I hope the guards let you park your car in the courtyard?'

'That's a matter for my chauffeur.'

Obviously! He was the sort of man who had a chauffeur and probably, in Bordeaux, a whole house full of servants.

'I imagine you know why I want to talk to you?'

'One of your inspectors mentioned Rue Notre-Dame-de-Lorette. I didn't understand what he was getting at.'

Maigret was sitting at his desk stuffing a pipe while the other man sat on a chair opposite him, facing the window.

'You knew Joséphine Papet.'

There was quite a long pause.

'I wonder how you were able to discover that.'

'As you must imagine, we have certain means of investigation, or else the prisons would be empty.'

'I don't appreciate your choice of words. If you are suggesting . . .'

'Not at all. Have you read this morning's paper?'

'Like everyone else.'

'So you know that Joséphine Papet, more familiarly known as Josée, was murdered yesterday afternoon in her apartment. Where were you?'

'Not at Rue Notre-Dame-de-Lorette, anyway.'

'Were you in your office?'

'At what time?'

'Let's say between three and four.'

'I was walking on the Grands Boulevards.'

'On your own?'

'Does that seem strange to you?'

'Do you often go walking like that?'

'When I'm in Paris, for an hour in the morning, at about ten, and an hour in the afternoon. My doctor will confirm that he's the one who recommended that I take some exercise. I used to be much fatter than I am now, and I was at risk of heart failure.'

'You realize that you have no alibi?'

'Do I need one?'

'Like Josée's other lovers.'

He didn't flinch, he remained imperturbable and simply asked:

'Were there many of us?'

There was a note of sarcasm in his voice.

'Four, to my knowledge, not counting the one who lived with her.'

'Because someone lived with her?'

'If my information is correct, your day was Saturday, because everyone had his day, more or less.'

'I have my habits. I follow a certain routine. On Saturday, after visiting Rue Notre-Dame-de-Lorette, I take the Bordeaux express so that I can be home by late evening.'

'Are you married, Monsieur Lamotte?'

'Married with children. One of my sons works with me, in our Bordeaux warehouses. Another is our representative in Bonn and takes frequent trips to the north. My son-in-law lives in London with my daughter and my two grandchildren.'

'Had you known Joséphine Papet for a long time?'

'Four years, more or less.'

'What did she mean to you?'

He said condescendingly, with a hint of contempt:

'A distraction.'

'You mean that you had no affection for her?'

'The word affection would seem to overstate the case.'

'Would fondness be more accurate?'

'She was pleasant company and she seemed discreet. So discreet that I'm surprised you've identified me. Can I ask you who gave you my name?'

'Someone mentioned a man with a limp who came on Saturday.'

'A riding accident when I was seventeen.'

'You have a railway season ticket.'

'I get it . . . Find the man with the Paris–Bordeaux season ticket who walks with a limp . . .'

'There's one thing that surprises me, Monsieur Lamotte. You stay at the Hôtel Scribe and you could meet plenty of pretty, available women in any of the bars nearby.'

The man from Chartrons did not back down, and answered the questions patiently, with a certain loftiness. Isn't Chartrons the Faubourg Saint-Germain of Bordeaux, the neighbourhood where one finds genuine dynasties?

For Lamotte, Maigret was a policeman. They were needed, certainly, to protect citizens' property, but this was the first time that he had come into contact with such people.

'What's your name again?'

'It doesn't matter. Maigret, if you insist.'

'First of all, Monsieur Maigret, I am an orderly man, a man who was brought up according to certain principles that barely apply these days . . . It is not my custom to visit bars. As strange as it may seem, I have never set foot in a café in Bordeaux, except when I was a student.

'As for bringing one of the women of whom you speak into my apartment at the Scribe, you must admit that it would be less than respectable, and that it would also present certain dangers.'

'Do you mean blackmail?'

'It's a risk in my position.'

'But you went to see Josée every week at Rue Notre-Dame-de-Lorette.'

'It was less risky, wasn't it?'

Maigret was growing impatient.

'And yet you knew nothing about her.'

'Would you rather I had come and asked you to investigate her?'

'Where did you first meet her?'

'In the restaurant car.'

'Was she going to Bordeaux?'

'Coming back. We found ourselves sitting opposite one another at a two-person table. She seemed very respectable, and when I offered her the bread basket she looked at me suspiciously at first. As it happened, we found ourselves in the same compartment.'

'Did you already have a mistress?'

'Don't you find the question impertinent, and entirely irrelevant to your inquiry?'

'Would you rather not answer?'

'I have nothing to hide from you. I did have one, one of my former secretaries, whom I had put up in a studio on Avenue de la Grande Armée. She had told me a week before that she was going to get married.'

'Creating a vacancy.'

'I don't appreciate your irony, and I am tempted not to answer your questions.'

'Then you would risk being kept here longer than you would wish.'

'Is that a threat?'

'A warning.'

'I won't take the trouble to call my lawyer. So ask away.'

He was becoming increasingly arrogant, increasingly curt.

'How long after meeting Josée did you go to Rue Notre-Dame-de-Lorette?'

'Three weeks. Perhaps a month.'

'Did she tell you she was working?'

'No.'

'What did she claim she lived on?'

'A small allowance left to her by one of her uncles.'

'And by the way, where did she tell you she came from?'

'From near Grenoble.'

It seemed that Joséphine Papet had the same need to tell lies as Florentin. To each man she had given a different place of birth.

'Did you give her a large monthly allowance?'

'That's not a very delicate question.'

'I would like you to reply.'

'I gave her two thousand francs every month, in an envelope, or rather I left it on the mantelpiece.'

Maigret smiled. He felt as if he had been taken back to his earliest days in the police, when one still saw old gentlemen on the Boulevards, wearing monocles and with polished shoes and white gaiters, following the pretty women.

It was a time of furnished mezzanines, of kept women, who must have been as gentle, discreet and good-humoured as Joséphine Papet.

Victor Lamotte was not in love. His life was in his family, in Bordeaux, in his austere house, the occasional weekdays at the Hôtel Scribe and in his offices on Rue Auber.

He still needed an oasis where he could drop his mask of respectability and talk openly. What risk could there be in letting himself go with a woman like Josée?

'You don't know any of the other visitors?'

'She didn't introduce them to me.'

'You might accidentally have found yourself face to face with one of them.'

'But that never happened.'

'Did you go out with her?'

'No.'

'Did your chauffeur wait in the street?'

He shrugged, as if he found Maigret very naive.

'I always went to see her by taxi.'

'You know she bought herself a building in Montmartre?'

'If you say so.'

These questions didn't concern him and left him indifferent.

'And forty-eight thousand francs were found in her apartment.'

'Part of that probably comes from me, but don't worry, I won't try and claim it back.'

'Were you affected by her death?'

'To tell the truth, no. Millions of people die every day.'

Maigret got to his feet. He had had enough. If he had continued this interrogation any longer he would have found it difficult to conceal his disgust.

'You're not going to make me sign a statement?'

'No.'

'Will I have to wait to be heard by the examining magistrate?'

'I can't yet answer that question.'

'If the case goes to court.'

'It will.'

'As long as you find the murderer.'

'We will find him.'

'I should warn you that I won't testify. I have friends in high places.'

'I have no doubt.'

And Maigret walked towards the door, which he held wide open. As he crossed the threshold, Lamotte turned round, hesitated to say goodbye and finally left without a word.

That made three! Leaving only the redhead. Maigret was in a bad mood and needed a bit of time to calm down. The rain had stopped long ago. A fly, perhaps the same one as yesterday, flew into the room as he sat down and began mechanically scribbling on a sheet of paper.

The scribbles turned into words.

Premeditation.

Unless the murderer was Florentin, premeditation was unlikely: the murderer had come without a weapon. It was someone who knew the victim, because he was aware that there was a loaded revolver in the bedside table.

In fact, wasn't he counting on that weapon?

Always supposing that Florentin was really in the wardrobe, why had the man spent nearly a quarter of an hour in the bedroom, where he couldn't pace about without stepping over the corpse?

Was it money that he was looking for? How had he managed not to find it, when all he had to do was force a drawer with a feeble lock?

Letters? Some kind of document?

None of them, neither François Paré, the civil servant, nor Fernand Courcel, the fat man, nor last of all the disdainful Victor Lamotte, needed money.

All three, on the other hand, would probably have reacted violently to blackmail.

He kept coming back to Florentin, Florentin whom the magistrate would have forced him to arrest if he had been aware of the facts.

Maigret had hoped to interrogate the red-haired man, Jean-Luc Bodard, but the inspector whom he had sent to find him had come back empty-handed. The young insurance salesman was away on a trip and wouldn't be back until the evening.

He lived in a small hotel on Boulevard des Batignolles, the Hôtel Beauséjour, and took his meals in restaurants.

Maigret was worried, as if something was going wrong with his investigation. He was unhappy with himself, uneasy. He didn't feel up to studying the files piled up on his desk and he opened the door to the inspectors' office.

'Come with me,' he said to Lapointe. 'We're going to take a car.'

It was only once they were on the embankment that he muttered:

'Rue Notre-Dame-de-Lorette.'

He felt as if he had forgotten an important point, as if he had overlooked the truth without realizing it. For the whole journey he didn't say a word and bit so hard on his pipe that he broke the ebonite stem.

'Park the car and then come and find me.'

'In the apartment?'

'In the lodge.'

He was haunted by the monstrous silhouette of the

concierge and her motionless eyes. He found her in exactly the same place as the day before, standing behind her tulle curtain, holding it aside with her hand, and she only decided to step back when he pushed the door open.

She didn't ask what he wanted and merely looked at him with disapproval.

Her skin was very white, an unhealthy white. Was she 'a bit slow' as they say in the countryside, one of those inoffensive simpletons that one used to come across in villages?

He grew impatient, seeing her standing stock still in the middle of the lodge.

'Sit down,' he said irritably.

She calmly shook her head.

'I asked you some questions yesterday and now I'm going to ask you them again. I should warn you this time that you could be prosecuted for giving false evidence if you don't tell the truth.'

She didn't flinch, and he thought he could see amusement in her eyes. She clearly wasn't afraid of him. She wasn't afraid of anybody.

'Did anyone go up to the third floor between three and four o'clock?'

'No.'

'And the other floors?'

'Only an old woman, to see the dentist.'

'Do you know François Paré?'

'No.'

'A big, fat man, in his fifties, balding and with a black moustache . . .'

'Perhaps.'

'He used to come here on Wednesday at about half past five. Did he come yesterday?'

'Yes.'

'At what time?'

'I don't know exactly. Before six.'

'Did he stay up there for a long time?'

'He came down straight away.'

'He didn't ask you any questions?'

'No.'

She answered mechanically, her face motionless, without taking her eyes off Maigret, as if she was still waiting for him to set a trap for her. Was it possible that she was protecting someone? Did she realize the importance of her statements?

It was the fate of Florentin that was at stake because, if no one had come into the house, the tale told by Maigret's childhood friend was false, there had been no ring on the door, no visitor, no waiting in the wardrobe, and Florentin had definitely shot his girlfriend.

There was a faint knock on the window, and Maigret brought in Lapointe.

'One of my inspectors,' he explained. 'Once again, weigh your words and only reply if you're certain.'

She had never played such an important part in her life, and she seemed to be cheering inwardly. It must have been marvellous to see a chief of police practically begging her to help him.

'Was François Paré never there during the afternoon?'

'No.'

'Are you sure that you'd have seen him?'

'Yes.'

'But sometimes you go into your kitchen.'

'Not at that time of day.'

'Where is the telephone?'

'In the kitchen.'

'If someone called . . .'

'No one called.'

'Does the name Courcel mean anything to you?'

'Yes.'

'Why do you know that name and not Monsieur Paré's?'

'Because he practically lived here. Ten years ago he
spent many of his nights up there, and he often went out
with the Papet girl.'

'Was he cordial towards you?'

'He said hello to me as he passed.'

'Did you like him better than the others?'

'He was more polite.'

'He still sometimes spends the night here on Thursday
evening.'

'That's none of my business.'

'He didn't come yesterday?'

'No.'

'Do you know his car?'

'It's blue.'

Her voice was neutral and toneless. Lapointe was startled by this phenomenon.

'Do you know the name of the man with the limp?'

'No.'

'He's never stopped in the lodge?'

'No.'

'He's called Lamotte. You didn't see him yesterday either?'

'No.'

'And you didn't see the red-haired man called Bodard?'

'I didn't see him.'

Maigret wanted to shake her to drag the truth out of her, like getting money out of a piggy-bank.

'In short, you are telling me that Léon Florentin stayed on his own up there with Joséphine Papet.'

'I didn't go up there.'

It was exasperating.

'But it's the only possible solution if we are to believe your evidence.'

'I can't help that.'

'Do you hate Florentin?'

'That's my business.'

'One might imagine that you were taking revenge.'

'Let people think what they will.'

There was a flaw somewhere, Maigret could feel it. Even if her immobility was natural to her, even if she normally spoke in that monotonous voice, using as few words as possible, something was wrong. Either she was lying deliberately, for some unknown reason, or she wasn't telling them everything she knew.

She was staying on the defensive, that much was certain, trying to second-guess the questions.

'Tell me, Madame Blanc . . . Did anyone threaten you?'

'No.'

'Maybe Joséphine Papet's murderer threatened to make you shut up if you talked.'

She shook her head.

'Let me finish . . . By speaking to us, you enable us to arrest him, and as a result he won't be able to do anything more to you. By remaining silent, you run the risk that he will consider it more prudent to get rid of you.'

Why the sudden irony on her face?

'A murderer will rarely hesitate to kill an awkward witness. I could cite you dozens of cases. But if you don't trust us, we won't be able to protect you . . .'

For a few seconds Maigret hoped. She didn't go so far as to become truly human, but there was something like a lapse, a slight tremor, perhaps a hesitation.

He waited anxiously.

'What do you have to say about it?' he said at last.

'Nothing.'

He was at the end of his tether.

'Come on, Lapointe.'

And, once he was in the street:

'I'm almost certain that she knows something . . . I wonder if she's as stupid as she seems.'

'Where are we going now?'

He hesitated. While waiting to question the insurance salesman, he no longer knew where to pick up the investigation.

'Boulevard Rochechouart.'

Florentin's studio was closed, and the painter working in the adjacent doorway called to them:

'There's nobody there.'

'Did he leave a long time ago?'

'He didn't come back for lunch. Are you from the police?'

'Yes.'

'I thought so. Since yesterday there's always been some-one roaming about in the courtyard and following him as soon as he goes out. What's he done?'

'We don't even know if he's done anything.'

'So he's a suspect!'

'If you like.'

He was a man who just wanted to talk, something that he probably missed during the day.

'Do you know him well?'

'We sometimes chatted.'

'Did he have a lot of customers?'

The painter gave Maigret a comical look.

'Customers? Well, first of all, where would they have come from? It wouldn't have occurred to anybody to turn up in this courtyard expecting to find an antiques shop. If you can call them antiques . . .

'Besides, he was rarely here. He hardly did anything but hang up a sign: "Back in a minute" or "Closed until Thursday".'

'Did he sometimes sleep in the storeroom?'

'I suppose so, because I sometimes saw him in the morning, shaving. I have lodgings on Rue Lamarck.'

'Did he ever confide in you?'

He thought this over, still wielding his brushes. He was so used to painting the Sacré-Coeur that he could have done it blindfolded.

'He doesn't like his brother-in-law, that's for certain.'

'Why?'

'He told me that if his brother-in-law hadn't stolen from

him, he wouldn't be where he is. His parents had a pros-perous business, I can't remember where . . .'

'In Moulins.'

'Could be. When his father retired, the daughter's hus-band took over the business. He was supposed to give some of the takings to Florentin. That was what they'd agreed. And yet once the father was dead he stopped pay-ing anything.'

Maigret remembered the pink, laughing girl who had stood behind the white marble counter and who, perhaps, was the real reason for his very rare visits to the patisserie.

'He never asked you for money?'

'How did you know? No large sums. Besides, I couldn't have lent him large sums. Twenty-five francs here and there, sometimes fifty, but rarely . . .'

'Did he pay you back?'

'Not the next day, as he promised, but a few days later . . . What's he suspected of? You're Detective Chief Inspector Maigret, aren't you? I recognized you immediately, because I've seen photographs of you in the papers.

'If you're taking the trouble to look into him, it must be an important case . . . A crime? Do you think he's killed somebody?'

'I haven't the faintest idea.'

'If you want to know my opinion, he's not someone who's capable of killing. I'm not saying he hasn't commit-ted the occasional indiscretion . . . And anyway! Perhaps it isn't his fault. He's always got new projects on the go, and I'm convinced that he believes in them. His ideas aren't always bad. Then he gets carried away and it comes to nothing.'

'You don't by any chance have a key to his studio?'

'How did you know?'

'Just a guess.'

'Customers only turn up once in a blue moon, and that's why he left me the key. I know the price of the few bits of furniture he has for sale.'

He went and fetched a large key from a drawer.

'I don't suppose he'll mind.'

'Don't worry.'

For the second time Maigret, helped by Lapointe, patiently searched the studio, then the storeroom. They left no corner unexplored. There was a sweetish smell in the storeroom, a shaving soap that Maigret wasn't familiar with.

'What are we looking for, chief?'

And Maigret muttered:

'I have no idea.'

'Nobody around Rue Notre-Dame-de-Lorette saw a blue Jaguar yesterday. A woman in the dairy knows the car very well.

' "It parks just outside the shop every Thursday . . . Hold on! Today's Thursday, and I haven't seen it . . . It's a little fat man who drives it. I hope nothing's happened to him." '

Janvier delivered his report.

'I also went to the garage on Rue La Bruyère. I saw the car registered in the name of Joséphine Papet. It's a two-year-old Renault. It has only twenty-four thousand kilometres on the clock and it's very well maintained. Nothing in the boot. In the glove compartment, a Michelin guide, a pair of sunglasses and a tube of aspirin.'

'I hope we'll have more luck with the insurance man.'

Janvier sensed that his boss was floundering and was careful to say nothing, maintaining an innocent expression.

'Have you called him in?' he asked at last, however.

'He doesn't get back to his hotel until the evening. You could go there, at about eight o'clock, for example. You might have a long time to wait. As soon as he arrives, call me at Boulevard Richard-Lenoir.'

It was after six. The offices were emptying. Just as he was about to pick up his hat, the phone rang. It was Inspector Leroy.

'I'm in a restaurant on Rue Lepic, chief, where he's eating. I'm going to do the same. We spent the afternoon in a cinema on Place Clichy which was showing some witless film. As it was a continuous performance, we saw the film through almost twice, sitting one behind the other.'

'Did he look worried?'

'Not at all. He turned round from time to time to glance at me. He nearly suggested joining him for something to eat.'

'I'll send someone to Boulevard Rochechouart shortly to take over from you.'

'You know, I'm not tired at all.'

'Send somebody along, Janvier. I don't know who's available. And don't forget to call me as soon as the redhead gets back to his hotel. The Beauséjour. It would be better if he doesn't know you're there.'

Maigret stopped on Place Dauphine to have a drink at the bar. The day had made a bad impression on him, particularly his conversation with Victor Lamotte.

The interview with the concierge certainly hadn't been any more inspiring.

'Give me another.'

He waved to some colleagues who were playing cards in a corner. When he got home, he made no attempt to conceal his bad mood. And with Madame Maigret that was impossible anyway.

'When I think how easy it would be!' he groaned, taking off his hat.

'What would be easy?'

'Arresting Florentin. That's what anyone would do in my place. If I told the examining magistrate about half the evidence I have against him, he'd send me to arrest him straight away.'

'Why are you hesitating? Because he was your friend?'

'Not my friend. A schoolmate,' he corrected her.

He filled a meerschaum pipe, one that he only smoked in the apartment.

'That's not why . . .'

He looked as if he himself was trying to find out the real reason for his attitude.

'Everything's against him. There's a bit too much against him, do you understand? And most of all I don't like the concierge.'

She almost burst out laughing, because he said it seriously, as if it was a serious argument.

'From where we are, we can't imagine the life that that girl led. As for the fellows who came to see her on particular days, it's almost impossible to believe . . .'

He was angry with everyone: with Joséphine Papet, first of all, for allowing herself to be killed so stupidly, with Florentin for accumulating all that incriminating evidence against himself, with that solemn civil servant Paré, whose wife suffered from nervous exhaustion, with the fat little ball-bearings man and particularly with that presumptuous limping man from Bordeaux.

But it was the concierge that he kept coming back to.

'She's lying . . . I'm sure that she's lying, or hiding something . . . Except that she's never going to give in.'

'Eat up.'

She had served a very frothy omelette aux fines herbes, and Maigret wasn't even paying it any attention. The salad was flavoured with croutons rubbed with garlic, followed by juicy peaches.

'You shouldn't take this business so much to heart.'

He looked at her like someone thinking about something else.

'What do you mean?'

'It's as if you're personally involved, as if it's a member of your family.'

He suddenly relaxed, realizing how ridiculous his attitude was, and smiled at last.

'You're right. It's stronger than me. I hate it when

people cheat. And yet someone's cheating, and it's getting to me.'

The phone rang.

'You see!'

'He's just gone into the hotel,' Janvier announced at the other end of the line.

It was the redhead's turn. Maigret was about to hang up when Janvier added:

'There's a woman with him.'

5.

Boulevard des Batignolles, with its lines of trees, was gloomy and deserted but, at its end, by contrast, Place Clichy could be seen brilliantly lit.

Janvier emerged from the shadows, the glowing tip of his cigarette piercing the darkness.

'They came on foot, arm in arm. The man is small, short legs, very lively. The girl is young and pretty.'

'You can go home to bed, or your wife will be cross with me.'

From the badly lit corridor Maigret recognized the smell because, when he had first arrived in Paris, he had stayed in a similar hotel in Montparnasse, the Hôtel de la Reine Morte. What queen did it refer to? No one had been able to tell him. The managers were from the Auvergne and they were fiercely determined that no one should cook in the rooms.

It was a smell of warm sheets, of human lives crammed together. The fake marble plaque outside announced, as at the Reine Morte:

> Rooms by the month,
> the week and the day.
> Every convenience.
> Bathrooms.

They neglected to mention that there was only one bath-room per floor, and that you had to queue to use it.

In the office he found a woman in slippers and a dressing gown, flaxen-haired, doing the day's accounts at a roll-top desk, with the key panel in front of her.

'Monsieur Bodard, please.'

She didn't look up and muttered:

'Fourth floor . . . Room 68.'

There was no lift. The stair carpet was threadbare, and the smell became more intense the higher one climbed. Maigret knocked at number 68, at the end of the corridor. No reply. After the third knock, a rather aggressive male voice said:

'Who is it?'

'I'd like to talk to Monsieur Bodard.'

'What about?'

'I'd rather not tell the whole hotel about it by shouting through the door.'

'Couldn't you come back another day?'

'It's quite urgent.'

'Who are you?'

'If you open the door a crack, I'll be able to tell you.'

There was a sound of bedsprings. The door half opened, and Maigret saw a shock of very curly red hair, a boxer's face, a naked body more or less hidden behind the door. Without a word he showed his badge.

'Are you going to take me away?' Bodard asked, without a hint of fear or anxiety in his voice.

'I just want to ask you some questions.'

'It's just that I'm not alone . . . You'll have to wait a few minutes.'

The door closed again. Maigret heard voices and feet moving about. More than five minutes passed before the door opened, by which time he had sat down on a step.

'Come in.'

The brass bed was unmade. A girl was finishing combing her dark hair at the mirror that hung above the dressing table. Maigret felt as if he had gone back thirty-five years, the setting was so reminiscent of the Reine Morte.

The girl wore a cotton dress, and her feet were bare in her sandals. She seemed to be in a bad mood.

'I suppose I've got to go out?'

'That would be preferable,' the red-haired man replied.

'When will I see you again?'

Bodard looked quizzically at Maigret.

'In an hour?'

The inspector nodded.

'Go and wait for me at the brasserie.'

She looked Maigret up and down with a far from benevolent eye, picked up her handbag and passed through the door.

'I'm sorry if I've come at a bad time.'

'I didn't expect you so quickly. I thought it would take you two or three days to track me down.'

He had just put on a pair of trousers. His torso was bare, a strong, muscular torso that compensated for his small height. His legs in particular were short. His feet were bare too.

'If you want to sit down . . .'

He himself sat down on the edge of the unmade bed,

and Maigret took a seat in the one armchair in the room, which was very uncomfortable.

'I expect you've read the paper?'

'Like everyone.'

He didn't seem mean. If he was cross with his visitor for interrupting a pleasant tête-à-tête, there was still a sense that he was good-natured, with bright eyes that expressed optimism. He wasn't a man to be weighed down, to take a tragic view of life.

'Is it really you, Maigret? I thought you would be fatter. And I didn't think detective chief inspectors went around knocking on doors.'

'It happens, as you see.'

'Of course, you've come to talk to me about poor Josée . . .'

He lit a cigarette.

'Have you arrested anyone yet?'

Maigret smiled, because so far it was the redhead who was asking the questions. Their roles were reversed.

'Did the concierge talk to you about me? She's not a woman, she's a monument, a funeral monument I would even say. She sends shivers down your spine.'

'How long did you know Joséphine Papet?'

'Wait . . . It's now June . . . It was the day after my birthday, so the 19th of April.'

'How did you meet her?'

'By ringing on her doorbell. That day I rang on all the doorbells in the building. That's my job, if you can call it a job. They must have told you: I sell insurance.'

'I know.'

'Each of us has two or three arrondissements, and we spend our days combing them.'

'Do you remember what day of the week it was?'

'A Thursday. Again, it's because of my birthday that I remember, and I had an awful hangover.'

'In the morning?'

'At about eleven.'

'Was she alone?'

'No. There was a big scrawny beanpole who said to the woman:

' "I'll be off."

'He looked at me closely and he left.'

'So you sell life insurance?'

'Accident insurance too. And savings insurance, a new thing that's enjoying a certain success. I haven't been in the branch for a long time. Before that I was a waiter in a café.'

'Why did you change jobs?'

'You said it: for a change. I've also been a fairground barker. It takes a lot more blarney than insurance, but insurance seems more respectable.'

'Mademoiselle Papet became your client?'

'Not in that sense.'

He laughed.

'In what sense?'

'I should tell you that she was in her dressing gown, with a headscarf over her hair, and there was a vacuum-cleaner in the middle of the room. I did my routine and all the while I was eyeing her up.

'She wasn't that young, but she was nicely rounded, and I had a sense that she thought I wasn't too bad either.

'She announced that she wasn't interested in life insurance, for the good reason that she had no heirs, and her money would go God knows where.

'Then I talked to her about capital insurance, a tidy sum that you get hold of at sixty or earlier in the case of accident or illness.'

'Did she bite?'

'She didn't say yes or no. Then, as usual, I tried my luck . . . There's nothing I can do about it. It's just how I am. Sometimes they get angry and give you a slap, but it's worth trying, even if it only works one time in three.'

'Did it work?'

'Like a dream.'

'How long have you known the young person who was here just now?'

'Olga? Since yesterday.'

'How did you meet her?'

'In a self-service restaurant. She's a shop assistant at Bon Marché. It's your fault that I didn't find out whether she was worth it . . .'

'How many times did you see Joséphine Papet again?'

'I didn't count them. Ten times? Twelve?'

'Did she give you a key?'

'No. I rang the bell.'

'She didn't fix you a day?'

'She just told me she was out on Saturday and Sunday. I asked her if the tall guy with the grey hair was her husband, and she told me he wasn't.'

'Did you see him again?'

'Twice.'

'Did you get a chance to talk to him?'

'I'm not sure he thought much of me. He gave me a bit of a dirty look and left as soon as I arrived.

' "Who is he?" I asked Josée.

'She told me:

' "Don't worry about him. He's a sad sack. I picked him up like a stray dog."

' "But you're sleeping with him?" '

' "I have to. I try not to make him suffer too much. Sometimes he wants to kill himself." '

Jean-Luc Bodard seemed sincere.

'You didn't meet any other men in her apartment?'

'No, that is to say I didn't see them. We agreed that if she had visitors she would only open the door a crack, I would talk about insurance and she would tell me she wasn't interested.'

'Did that happen?'

'Two or three times.'

'What day of the week?'

'There's a question . . . What I do know is that once it was a Wednesday.'

'At what time?'

'Four o'clock? Four thirty?'

Wednesday was Paré's day. And yet the man from Navigable Waterways had told him he never went to Rue Notre-Dame-de-Lorette before half past five or six o'clock.

'Did he see you?'

'I don't think so. The door was barely open a crack.'

Worried, Maigret studied him carefully.

'What do you know about her?'

'Let's think . . . She barely mentioned it . . . I think she was born in Dieppe.'

She hadn't lied to the redhead. The local chief inspector had called Dieppe about the funeral and the will. The woman named as Joséphine Papet had indeed been born in that town thirty-four years earlier, to a certain Hector Papet, a fisherman, and Léontine Marchaud, a housewife. She was not known to have any other family in the town.

Why had she told Bodard the truth, when she had given the others different places of birth?

'She spent some time working in a nightclub before meeting a wealthy man, an industrialist who lived with her for several months.'

'She didn't tell you what she lived on?'

'More or less. Rich friends came to see her from time to time.'

'Did you know their names?'

'No. But she confided in me, for example:

' "The man with the limp is starting to get on my nerves. If it wasn't for the fact that he scares me a little . . ." '

'She was afraid of him?'

'She was never entirely at ease, and that's why she kept a gun in the drawer of her bedside table.'

'Did she show it to you?'

'Yes.'

'She wasn't afraid of you?'

'Are you joking? Who would be afraid of me?'

And it was true that his face inspired sympathy. There was even something reassuring about his red curly hair, his almost violet eyes, his thick torso and his little short legs. He didn't look as old as thirty and he would probably always have the appearance of a young boy.

'Did she give you presents?'

He got up and walked to the chest of drawers, from which he took a silver cigarette case.

'This.'

'Never any small sums of money?'

'Come on!'

He was vexed, almost furious.

'It's my job to ask unpleasant questions.'

'Did you ask the same one to that great beanpole?'

'You mean Florentin?'

'I didn't know his name was Florentin. That one, yes, he was a kept man.'

'Did she talk to you about him?'

'You bet!'

'I thought she loved him.'

'At first, perhaps. She was glad to have someone to talk to, someone who didn't matter, someone she could do anything in front of. Usually, single women have a dog, a cat, a canary . . . You see what I mean?

'Except that big fellow Florentin, if that's his name, was playing her for a fool . . .'

'In what way?'

'When I met him, he said he was an antiques dealer. He was skint, but he was forever expecting his ship to come in the next day. Sometimes he bought old bits of furniture and did them up. Then he got used to doing nothing.

' "When I get my two hundred thousand francs . . ." he would say over and over.

'And he would extract a few ten-franc notes from her.'

'Why didn't she leave him if she'd stopped loving him?'

'You see, she was sentimental in a way people only are in romantic novels. Look! I told you what happened the first time we met. She was no longer a girl. She had experience, right? But afterwards she started sobbing.

'I didn't understand why, and I had found somewhere else to sit when she said, between two hiccups:

' "You're going to despise me . . ."

'You read that in old books, but it was the first time I'd heard a woman use those words . . .

'Florentin had worked it out. When he felt she'd had enough, he became even more sentimental than she was, he played out heartrending scenes. Sometimes he would leave, swearing that he wouldn't come back, that she'd never hear from him again, and she went to find him in some hovel he had kept on Boulevard Rochechouart.'

Maigret wasn't surprised by the portrait that was being drawn for him of his old classmate. Florentin had done the same thing when they threatened to throw him out of school. The unlikely rumour had circulated that he had literally hung on to the headmaster's coat-tails, swearing that he would never survive the dishonour.

'Another time, he took the gun out of the bedside table and pretended to aim at his temple . . .

' "You are my last love, and I will only have you in my life . . ."

'You know the refrain. For hours, days, she believed him. He got his self-confidence back, and she would start growing suspicious again.

'Basically, I think that she clung on to him because she had no one to replace him and she was afraid of being lonely.'

'And then she met you.'

'Yes.'

'She saw you as a possible replacement.'

'I think so. She asked me if I still had lots of girlfriends, if I felt any affection for her.

'She didn't throw her arms around my neck. It was subtler than that. A word from time to time.

' "You don't think I'm too old?"

'And, when I protested:

' "I'm five years older than you, and a woman ages faster than a man. Soon I'll have wrinkles . . ."

'Then she talked to me again about the tall thin fellow who considered himself more and more at home.

' "He wants me to marry him." '

Maigret shuddered.

'She said that to you?'

'Yes. She added that she owned a house, that she had set some money aside, that he had suggested buying a bar or a little restaurant near Porte Maillot.

'When he spoke of me it was with contempt. He called me the redhead, or shorty.

' "You'll see, he'll end up running rings around you . . ." '

'Tell me, Bodard, did you go to Rue Notre-Dame-de-Lorette yesterday afternoon?'

'I get it, inspector. You want me to come up with an alibi. Sadly, I haven't got one. For a while I had no girls apart from Josée, and I admit that she wasn't enough for me. Yesterday morning I sold a major policy to a seventy-year-old man who was worried about his future.

'The older they get, the more they worry about the future.

'Then, since the sun was shining, and I'd got a good lunch inside me, I decided to go on the prowl.

'I went down to the Boulevards and moved from bar to bar. It didn't start very well, but in the end I happened on Olga, the girl you saw, and who's waiting in a brasserie three buildings down from here. I didn't meet her until about seven o'clock. Until then, I have no alibi.'

He added with a laugh:

'Are you going to arrest me?'

'No. So, in short, Florentin had been in a precarious situation for a few weeks?'

'That is to say, if I'd wanted to, I could have taken his place, but I wasn't tempted.'

'Did he know?'

'He scented competition, I'm sure, because he's not an idiot. Besides, Josée must have alluded to the situation.'

'If he'd had to bump somebody off, logically it should have been you.'

'That sounds right. He couldn't have known that I had decided to say no and, little by little, to drop that woman. I can't bear women who blub.'

'Do you think he killed her?'

'I don't know, and it's none of my business. Besides, I don't know the others. One of them may have been angry with her for some reason or another.'

'Thank you.'

'Don't mention it . . . Hang on, I don't fancy getting dressed again. When you go past, could you tell that girl the coast is clear and she can come back up?'

It was the first time that Maigret had ever had to play such a part, but the request was delivered so naturally, so pleasantly, that he couldn't refuse.

'Goodnight.'

'Let's hope so.'

He found the brasserie, where the regulars were playing cards. It was an old, badly lit establishment, and the waiter smiled ironically when he saw Maigret making his way towards the girl.

'I'm sorry I stayed so long. He's waiting for you.'

Completely taken aback, she couldn't find anything to say, and he headed for the door and had to go back up to Place Clichy to find a taxi.

Maigret hadn't been mistaken when he thought that Page, the examining magistrate, had recently been promoted to the job in Paris. His office was on the top floor of the Palais de Justice, which hadn't yet been modernized. One might have thought that everything in it was a century old, and the atmosphere recalled the novels of Balzac.

The clerk was working on a white wooden kitchen table. He had covered it with wrapping paper fixed with drawing pins, and the airless office which should have been his, and which could be glimpsed through the half-open door, was filled with stacks of files up to the ceiling.

Maigret had called a little earlier to find out whether the magistrate was free and he had been told to come up.

'Take this chair. It's the best one. Or rather the least bad. It used to be part of a pair, but the other one collapsed last week under a witness weighing a hundred kilos.'

'May I?' Maigret asked, lighting his pipe.

'Please go ahead.

'Inquiries to try and trace Joséphine Papet's relatives have remained fruitless, and we can't leave her at the Forensic Institute for ever. It may take weeks or months before we dig up a second cousin or a cousin once removed. Don't you think that we could move on to the funeral tomorrow, for example?'

'Since she had a certain amount of property.'

'I deposited the forty-eight thousand francs that you gave me at the Registry, because I don't trust the lock on my office.'

'If you'll permit me, I'll contact an undertaker.'

'Was she Catholic?'

'Léon Florentin, who lived with her, claims she wasn't. At any rate, she never went to mass.'

'Have them send me the bill. I don't know exactly how that works from the administrative point of view. Will you record that, Dubois?'

'Yes, sir.'

The unpleasant moment had arrived. Maigret hadn't tried to avoid it. On the contrary, it was he who had requested this meeting.

'I didn't send you a report, because I'm still not certain.'

'You suspect the friend she lived with? What was his name again?'

'Florentin. I have every reason to suspect him, and yet I'm still hesitating. It strikes me as too easy. And besides, it so happens that I went to school with him in Moulins. He's an intelligent fellow, more perspicacious than the average.

'If he hasn't succeeded in life, it's because of a particular turn of mind that prevents him from accepting any kind of discipline. I'm convinced that he thinks he lives in a world of puppets, and that he refuses to take anything seriously.

'He has a police record . . . Bad cheques . . . Fraud . . . He spent a year in prison, but I still think he's incapable of killing. Or rather, he would have made sure that he didn't come under suspicion.

'I have him under surveillance day and night.'

'Does he know?'

'He's flattered and, in the street, he turns round from time to time to glance at the man tailing him. He was the class joker. You must have experienced that kind of thing.'

'There's one in every class.'

'Except that at fifty they aren't funny any more. I've traced Joséphine Papet's other lovers. One is a fairly senior civil servant whose wife suffers from nervous exhaustion. The two others are rich and highly thought of, one in Bordeaux, the other in Rouen.

'Of course, each of them thought he was the only one who visited the apartment on Rue Notre-Dame-de-Lorette.'

'Did you disabuse them?'

'Not only did I disabuse them, I had summonses delivered into their own hands for a confrontation that will take place at three o'clock in my office.

'I've also summoned the concierge, because I'm sure she's hiding something from me. I hope to be able to tell you more tomorrow.'

A quarter of an hour later, Maigret was in his office and had put Lucas in charge of organizing the funeral. And handing him a banknote, he added:

'Take this. Make sure there are some flowers.'

In spite of the sun, as bright as it had been on the previous days, it was impossible to open the window because of the strong wind that was shaking the branches of the trees.

The ones who had received a summons for the afternoon must have been worried sick, not suspecting that Maigret was the most anxious of all. He had relaxed a little when talking to the examining magistrate. But that didn't mean that he wasn't torn by conflicting emotions.

Two characters kept attracting his attention: Florentin, of course, who seemed to have taken a sly pleasure in accumulating clues against himself, and then that nightmarish concierge whose image haunted him. Where she was concerned, he had decided to have her brought in by an inspector, because she would have been quite capable of not showing up.

To stop thinking about it, he spent the rest of the morning going through his backlog of files and immersed himself so fully in his work that he was surprised to see that it was ten to one.

He called Boulevard Richard-Lenoir to tell his wife that he wouldn't be coming home for lunch, went to the Brasserie Dauphine and sat down in his corner. Several of his colleagues were at the bar. There were also some people from the Vice Squad and Special Branch.

'We've got veal ragout,' the landlord came and told him. 'Will that do?'

'Perfect.'

'And a carafe of our rosé?'

He ate slowly, amid the hubbub of conversations punctuated by the occasional peal of laughter. Then he calmly drank his coffee along with the little glass of calvados that the landlord invariably gave him.

At 2.45, he went and got some chairs from the inspectors' office and arranged them in a semi-circle.

'Have you got that, Janvier? You go and get her. You keep her in an empty office and don't bring her to me until I call you.'

'Do you think we'll get all of her in the car?' the inspector joked.

The first to arrive was Jean-Luc Bodard. He was vibrant and full of beans. But when he saw the chairs lined up, he frowned.

'Is this a family reunion or a board meeting?'

'A bit of both.'

'You mean that you're going to assemble everyone who . . .'

'Exactly.'

'Fine by me. Can't wait to see their faces, can you?'

At that point one of them was brought in by old Joseph, and looked glumly around.

'I was given your summons, but I wasn't told.'

'You won't be alone, in fact. Have a seat, Monsieur Paré.'

He was dressed entirely in black, as he had been the previous day, his bearing was stiffer than it had been in his office, and he kept darting anxious glances at the red-haired man.

There was a pause of two or three minutes during which not a word was uttered. François Paré was sitting beside the window with his black hat on his knees. Jean-Luc Bodard, wearing a sports jacket with a wide check, looked at the door and waited to see the new arrivals coming in.

Next was Victor Lamotte, who was actually bridling, and who asked Maigret in a furious voice:

'Is this a trap?'

'Please sit down.'

Maigret was playing the role of host, impassively and with a faint smile.

'You have no right to.'

'You can complain in high places later, Monsieur Lamotte. Meanwhile please take a seat.'

An inspector brought in Florentin, who was no less surprised than the others but who reacted with an explosion of laughter.

'Of all the things . . .!'

He looked at Maigret and winked at him knowingly. For someone who liked practical jokes, wasn't this one up to scratch?

'Gentlemen . . .' he said, saluting with mock solemnity.

And he took a chair near Lamotte, who moved his own as far away as he could in order to avoid contact.

Maigret looked at the clock. It had just struck three when Fernand Courcel appeared in the doorway, so surprised that his first reaction was to turn on his heels.

'Come in, Monsieur Courcel. Sit down. I think this is everybody.'

Young Lapointe at one end of the office was standing by to jot down anything that might be considered interesting.

Maigret sat down, lit his pipe and murmured:

'Of course, you can smoke.'

Only the redhead lit a cigarette. It was strange to see them all assembled like that, so different from one another. In fact they formed two groups. On the one hand, the two real lovers, Florentin and Bodard, who kept glancing at one another. The incumbent and the successor, in fact. The old and the new.

Did Florentin know that the redhead had almost taken his place? He didn't seem to resent him and looked at him with something like sympathy.

The three in the other group were more serious, the ones who had insisted on coming to Rue Notre-Dame-de-Lorette in search of some kind of illusion.

They had never seen one another, and yet none of them deigned to look at his neighbour.

'Gentlemen, you know, I suppose, why I have brought you all here. I have had the opportunity to question you separately, and to inform you about the situation.

'There are five of you and, for a longer or shorter period of time, you have all had intimate relations with Joséphine Papet.'

He waited for a moment and no one moved.

'Apart from Florentin and, to some extent, Monsieur Bodard, none of you was aware of the existence of the others. Is that correct?'

Only the redhead nodded. Florentin seemed to be highly amused.

'The fact is that Joséphine Papet is dead, and one of you killed her.'

Monsieur Lamotte rose from his seat and began:

'I protest against . . .'

It looked as if he was about to leave.

'You can protest later. Sit down. I haven't yet accused anyone and I've only determined a fact. All of you but one claim not to have set foot in the apartment on Wednesday between three and four o'clock. And none of you has an alibi.'

Paré raised his hand.

'No, Monsieur Paré. Yours doesn't hold up. I sent one of my men to check your office again. A second door leads on to a corridor which allows you to leave without being seen by your colleagues. And if your colleagues find that you aren't in your office, they assume you must be with the minister.'

Maigret relit his pipe, which had gone out in the meantime.

'I don't expect one of you to stand up and confess your guilt. I'm just telling you my ulterior motive: I'm sure not only that the murderer is here, but there is also someone who knows and is saying nothing for a reason that escapes me.'

He looked at each of them in turn. Florentin's eyes were turned towards the middle of the row, but there was no way of knowing who he was so interested in.

Victor Lamotte was hypnotized by his shoes. His face was pale, and his features looked as if they were caving in.

Courcel, who was trying to smile, managed only quite a pitiful grimace.

The redhead was thinking. Clearly Maigret's last few words had struck him, and he was trying to get his thoughts in order.

'Whoever the killer was, he was known to Josée, because she received him in her bedroom. And yet she wasn't alone in the apartment.'

This time they looked at one another, then they all turned suspiciously towards Florentin.

'That's right. Léon Florentin was there when the door-bell was rung, and since that had happened several times, he went and hid in the wardrobe.'

Maigret's ex-classmate struggled to maintain an attitude of indifference.

'Did you hear a man's voice, Monsieur Florentin?'

He could hardly address him as an old friend under these circumstances.

'You can't hear easily from the wardrobe. Only a murmur.'

'What happened?'

'After about a quarter of an hour a shot rang out.'

'Did you run?'

'No.'

'Did the murderer flee?'

'No.'

'How much longer did he stay in the apartment?'

'About a quarter of an hour.'

'Did he take the forty-eight thousand francs that were in the desk drawer?'

'No.'

Maigret didn't consider it necessary to add that it was in fact Florentin who had tried to appropriate the money.

'So the murderer was looking for something. I imagine that some of you must sometimes have written to Josée, during the holidays, for example, or to apologize for missing one of your appointments.'

He looked at them one by one again, and they crossed or uncrossed their legs.

Now he concentrated on the serious lovers, the ones with a family, a situation, a reputation to defend.

'Did you ever write to her, Monsieur Lamotte?'

He muttered a barely audible 'yes'.

'In Bordeaux you live in a milieu that has barely evolved over time, isn't that so? If I am well informed, your wife has a large personal fortune, and her family is rated more highly than yours on the scale of values of Chartrons. Has someone threatened you with a scandal?'

'I will not permit you to . . .'

'And you, Monsieur Paré . . . Did you ever write?'

'During the holidays, in fact . . .'

'In spite of your visits to Rue Notre-Dame-de-Lorette, I think you are very attached to your wife.'

'She's ill . . .'

'I know. I'm sure you wouldn't want to afflict her further.'

He clenched his jaws, on the brink of tears.

'And what about you, Monsieur Courcel?'

'If I wrote, it was only ever short notes.'

'Which still establish your relationship with Joséphine Papet . . . Your wife is younger than you, probably jealous . . .'

'And me?' the redhead asked comically.

'You might have had another reason to kill.'

'Wouldn't have been jealousy, anyway,' he announced, looking at the row of other men.

'Josée might have talked to you about her savings. If she told you that she didn't put them in the bank, but kept them in the apartment.'

'I would have taken them, I suppose?'

'Unless your search was interrupted.'

'Do I look like that kind of person?'

'Most of the murderers I've known looked like honest people . . . As for the letters, you could have taken them to blackmail their senders.

'Because the letters have disappeared, all the letters, possibly even including those from people we aren't aware of. It is rare to have reached the age of thirty-five without accumulating a more or less voluminous correspondence . . . And yet, in the desk, we found only bills.

'Your letters, gentlemen, have been taken, and by one of you.'

In trying not to look guilty, they assumed postures so unnatural that they immediately looked suspicious.

'I'm not asking the murderer to stand up and confess. Over the next few hours, I expect that the person who knows will show his face.

'Perhaps that won't be necessary, because we still have one witness to hear, and that witness knows the guilty man . . .'

Maigret turned towards Lapointe.

'Will you tell Janvier?'

The wait passed in total silence, and everyone avoided making the slightest movement. All of a sudden it was very hot, and the entrance of Madame Blanc, more monumental than ever, had a certain theatrical quality.

With a spinach-green dress she wore a red hat perched on the top of her head and held in her hand a bag almost as big as a suitcase. She had stopped just in front of the doorway and, stony-faced and blank-eyed, she looked around the assembled people.

Eventually, she turned back towards the door, and Janvier had to stop her making for the stairs. For a moment it looked as if they were about to wrestle with each other.

In the end she gave in and stepped into the office.

'I still have nothing to say,' she said with a nasty look at Maigret.

'Do you know these gentlemen?'

'I'm not paid to do your job. I want to go.'

'Which of them did you see, between three and four o'clock on Wednesday, making their way towards the lift or the stairs?'

At that moment something unexpected happened. That stubborn-looking woman, her face still impassive, wasn't quite able to hold back something that looked like a smile. Without any doubt, her face bore an expression of satisfaction, almost a sign of victory.

All eyes were on her. But which of them seemed most anxious? Maigret couldn't have said. They all reacted differently. Victor Lamotte was pale with suppressed rage, unlike Fernand Courcel, whose face had turned purple. As to François Paré, he was crippled with sadness and shame.

'Are you refusing to answer?' Maigret murmured at last.

'I have nothing to say.'

'Record that statement, Lapointe.'

She shrugged and said disdainfully, still with a hint of mystery in her voice:

'You don't scare me.'

6.

Maigret, now standing up and looking at each of them in turn, said:

'Gentlemen, thank you for coming. I think that this meeting will prove not to have been pointless, and that one of you will soon be in touch with me.'

He coughed lightly to clear his throat.

'It remains to me to tell you, in case you are interested, that Joséphine Papet's funeral will be held at ten o'clock tomorrow. The body will be collected from the Forensic Institute.'

Victor Lamotte was the first to leave, furious, without looking at anyone and, of course, without saying goodbye to Maigret. His limousine and his chauffeur would be waiting down below.

Courcel hesitated before merely nodding, while François Paré murmured as he passed, not really knowing what he was saying:

'Thank you.'

Only the redhead held out his hand and said cheerfully:

'Spot on! You gave them hell.'

Only Florentin lingered, and Maigret said to him:

'I'd like you to wait here for a moment. I'll be back shortly.'

He left him under the eye of Lapointe, who had not

moved from his place at the end of the office, and went into the inspectors' room. Torrence's large figure was there, typing out a report. He typed with two fingers, and with a look of great concentration.

'Go and organize a stake-out in front of the house on Rue Notre-Dame-de-Lorette. I need to know who goes in and who comes out. If one of the people leaving my office should turn up there, follow him inside.'

'Are you afraid of something?'

'The concierge may know too much, and I wouldn't want anything bad to happen to her.'

'Shall we go on following Florentin and put a guard in his courtyard?'

'Yes. I'll let you know when I'm done with him.'

He returned to his office.

'You can go, Lapointe.'

Florentin was standing by the window, hands in his pockets, as if he was at home. He displayed his usual irony.

'My goodness, how rattled they were! I've never had so much fun in my life.'

'You think so?'

Because his former classmate's cheerfulness was clearly forced.

'The one who took me aback was the concierge. It's not going to be easy to get anything out of her. Do you think she knows?'

'I hope so for your sake.'

'What do you mean?'

'She claims no one went up there between the hours of three and four. If she sticks to that position, I will be obliged to arrest you, because you will automatically become the only possible culprit.'

'Why did you make her appear in front of those men?'

'In the hope that one of them will be afraid that she might talk.'

'Aren't you afraid on my behalf too?'

'Did you see the murderer?'

'I've already told you I didn't.'

'Did you recognize his voice?'

'I've told you I didn't do that either.'

'So what are you afraid of?'

'I was in the apartment. You've told them. The man might believe that I've spotted him.'

Maigret carelessly opened a drawer in his desk and took out a packet of photographs that Moers had sent down from Criminal Records. He chose one which he held out to Florentin.

'Look.'

The son of the Moulins pastry-chef studied the photograph carefully, pretending not to understand why he had been given this document to examine. The picture showed part of the room, the bed and the bedside table with the half-open drawer.

'What am I supposed to see in particular?'

'Does nothing strike you?'

'No.'

'Remember your first statement. There was a ring at the door. You hurried towards the wardrobe.'

'That's the truth.'

'Right. Let us assume that it is the truth. According to

you, Josée and her visitor only stayed in the sitting room for a few moments. Passing through the dining room, they entered the bedroom.'

'That's what they did . . .'

'Wait. According to you they stayed there for almost a quarter of an hour before the shot was fired.'

Florentin looked again at the photograph, frowning.

'This picture was taken shortly after the murder, when nothing in the room had been touched . . . Look at the bed . . .'

A slight blush came to Florentin's thin cheeks.

'Not only has the bed not been unmade, but the bed-cover isn't even creased.'

'What are you getting at?'

'Either the visitor only came to talk to Josée, in which case they stayed in the sitting room, or he was there for some other reason, and we wouldn't have found the bed in that state. Would you like to tell me what they could have been doing in the bedroom?'

'I don't know.'

He was visibly trying to think quickly, to find an answer.

'Just now you were talking about letters.'

'So?'

'He might have come to demand his letters back.'

'And do you think Josée would have refused to give them to him? Do you think it likely she would blackmail a man who was bringing her a substantial monthly income?'

'Perhaps they went into the bedroom for some other reason and then argued.'

'Listen to me, Florentin. I know your statements by heart. From the first day I've felt that something was off. Did you take the letters just as you took the forty-eight thousand francs?'

'I swear I didn't. Where would I have put them? You've found the money, haven't you? If I'd had the letters, I would have hidden them in the same place.'

'Not necessarily. We patted your pockets to check that you didn't have the revolver, but we didn't search you thoroughly. You're an excellent swimmer, I remember. And yet you suddenly threw yourself into the Seine . . .'

'I'd had enough. I felt that you suspected me. And I'd just lost the only person in the world who . . .'

'Stop that, will you? Drop the act.'

'When I climbed over the parapet, I really wanted to end it all. Perhaps I wasn't thinking. One of those men was following me.'

'Exactly.'

'Exactly what?'

'Imagine you'd gone to hide the money on top of the wardrobe, and you didn't think about the letters. So they were still in your pocket. It would have been dangerous for you if they were found in your possession. How would you have explained it?'

'I don't know.'

'You suspected that the surveillance would continue. A dive into the Seine, as if in a fit of despair, and you would get rid of those papers, which would be kept at the bottom by some object, a stone, anything . . .'

'I didn't have the letters.'

'That's a possibility too, which would explain why, if you have been telling the truth, the murderer spent almost a quarter of an hour in the apartment. Except there's one detail that's troubling me.'

'What new clue have you found?'

'The fingerprints.'

'If my fingerprints have been found all over the place, that's to be expected, isn't it?'

'That's just the point, we didn't find them in the bedroom. Or anyone else's prints for that matter. And yet you opened the desk to take out the money. The murderer opened one of the drawers to take out the letters. He couldn't have spent a quarter of an hour in a room without touching anything.'

'So after he left you carefully wiped all the smooth surfaces, including the door-handles.'

'I don't understand. I didn't wipe anything. What is there to prove that no one came in while I was running home, and then went to see you at the Police Judiciaire?'

Maigret didn't reply and, seeing that the wind had subsided, went and opened the window. He left a long pause and then murmured:

'When were you going to clear the place?'

'What place? What do you mean?'

'Leave the apartment . . . Leave Josée, who you were living off.'

'There was never any question of that.'

'Yes, there was, as you know very well. She was starting to think that you were getting a bit past your best, and perhaps also a bit too greedy.'

'Is it that bastard of a redhead who told you that?'

'It doesn't matter.'

'It could only be him. He's been trying to weasel his way into the house for weeks.'

'He has a job. He earns a living.'

'So do I.'

'Your job is a fake job. How many pieces of furniture do you sell in a year? Most of the time there's a sign on your door saying you're not there.'

'I'm out and about, buying merchandise.'

'No. Joséphine Papet was slowly finding she'd had enough. She was counting, wrongly in fact, on Bodard to take your place.'

'It's his word or mine.'

'Yours isn't worth a cent. I've been aware of that since school.'

'You resent me, don't you?'

'Why would I resent you?'

'You already resented me in Moulins. My parents had a good business. I had money in my pocket. Your father was only ever a kind of servant at the Chateau of Saint-Fiacre.'

Maigret flushed, clenched his fists and nearly lashed out, because if there was one thing he wouldn't permit it was anyone touching the memory of his father. He had been estate manager at the chateau, and had been responsible for over twenty farms.

'You're a lowlife, Florentin.'

'You were asking for that.'

'I'm not putting you in jail yet, for lack of formal evidence, but I'll find it before long.'

He opened the door to the inspectors' office.

'Who's dealing with this scoundrel?'

Lourtie got to his feet.

'Stick to him closely and, when he goes home, go and stand outside his door. Arrange for a colleague to take over from you.'

Florentin, sensing that he had gone too far, murmured humbly:

'I'm sorry, Maigret. I lost my cool and didn't know what I was saying. Put yourself in my place.'

Maigret kept his teeth clenched and didn't watch him go when he left the office. The telephone rang a few moments later. It was the examining magistrate inquiring about the result of their meeting.

'I can't say yet,' Maigret replied. 'It's like when you go fishing; I've stirred up the bottom but I don't know what's going to come out of it. The funeral is at ten o'clock tomorrow.'

Some journalists were waiting in the corridor, and Maigret's manner was less amiable than usual.

'Are you following a lead, inspector?'

'I've got several.'

'And you don't know which is the right one?'

'Exactly.'

'Do you think it's a crime of passion?'

He nearly told them that there are no such things as crimes of passion. And yet that was more or less what he believed. He had learned in the course of his career that the spurned lover or the abandoned wife will kill less out of love than out of wounded pride.

That evening Madame Maigret watched television, and he had two little glasses of raspberry eau-de-vie that his sister-in-law had sent them from Alsace.

'Are you enjoying the film?'

He stopped himself from saying:

'What film?'

He saw images moving across the screen, people getting worked up, but he couldn't have said what was happening.

The next day, just before ten, he had Janvier drive him to the Forensic Institute.

Florentin, long and thin, a cigarette dangling from his lips, was standing on the edge of the pavement in the company of Bonfils, the inspector who had taken over Lourtie's shift.

Florentin didn't approach the police car. He stayed there, his shoulders slumped, like a humiliated man who doesn't dare to raise his head.

The hearse had arrived, and the people from the undertaker's brought the coffin on a bier.

Maigret opened the back door.

'Get in!'

And to Bonfils:

'You can go back to headquarters. I'll bring him to you.'

'Can we go?' the master of ceremonies asked.

They set off and, in the rear-view mirror, Maigret noticed a yellow car following them. It was a two-seater convertible, cheap, with dented bodywork, and Jean-Luc Bodard's red hair appeared above the windscreen.

They drove in silence towards Ivry, and passed through

the huge cemetery. The grave was ready in a new section where the trees had not yet had time to grow. Lucas hadn't forgotten Maigret's recommendation about flowers, and the redhead had brought a bouquet of his own.

As the coffin was being lowered, Florentin hid his face with both hands, and his shoulders twitched a few times. Was he crying? It made no difference, because he was capable of crying to order.

Maigret was invited to throw in the first spadeful of soil, and a few moments later the two cars were driving along the road again.

'To the Police Judiciaire, chief?'

He nodded. Behind him, Florentin was still silent.

In the courtyard of Quai des Orfèvres, Maigret got out and said to Janvier:

'Stay with him for a moment. I'm going to send out Bonfils, who will take him in.'

An impassioned voice reached him from the back of the car:

'I swear, Maigret, I didn't kill her . . .'

Maigret merely shrugged and, passing through the glass door, slowly climbed the stairs. He found Bonfils in the inspectors' office.

'Your client is downstairs. You're to take charge of him.'

'What do I do if he insists on walking beside me again?'

'Do whatever you like, but don't lose him.'

He was surprised, upon entering his office, to find Lapointe waiting for him with a concerned expression.

'Bad news, chief . . .'

'Another corpse?'

'No. The concierge has disappeared.'

'I'd ordered her to be kept under surveillance.'

'Lourtie phoned half an hour ago . . . He's so rattled that there was a sob in his voice . . .'

He was one of the old inspectors, one of the most conscientious, who knew the job inside out.

'How did that happen?'

'Lourtie was on the pavement opposite when the woman left the building, without a hat, holding a bag of groceries.

'Without looking behind her to see if she was being followed, first of all she went into a butcher's shop where they seemed to know her and bought a chop.

'Still without turning round, she continued on down Rue Saint-Georges and this time she went into an Italian grocer's shop, while Lourtie paced up and down outside.

'After a quarter of an hour or so, he started to worry. He went into the long, narrow shop to find another entrance leading on to the Square d'Orléans and Rue Taitbout . . . Of course, the bird had flown.

'Lourtie called us and then, rather than pointlessly combing the area, returned to his stake-out in front of the house . . . Do you think she's fled?'

'Certainly not.'

Maigret had returned to his place by the window and was looking at the leaves of the chestnut trees, where birds were chirping.

'Since she wasn't the one who killed Joséphine Papet, she has no reason to flee, particularly dressed as she was, with a bag of groceries on her arm.

'She had someone to meet . . . I'm almost sure that she made her decision after the confrontation yesterday.

'And yet I've always been sure that she'd seen the murderer, either going up or coming down, or both times . . .

'Suppose that when he was leaving the man found her with her nose pressed against the glass, her eyes fixed on him . . .'

'I'm starting to understand.'

'He knew she would be questioned. But he was a regular visitor to Joséphine Papet, and the concierge knew him.'

'Do you think he threatened her?'

'She wasn't the kind of woman to be easily intimidated. You may have noticed that yesterday afternoon. On the other hand, I can see that she might easily be seduced by money.'

'If she received money, why disappear?'

'Because of the meeting.'

'I don't understand.'

'The murderer was there. She saw him. She only had to say a word to have him arrested. She chose to remain silent. Then I would bet that she understood that her silence was worth a lot more than what she had received . . .

'That morning she decided to go and demand a top-up, but she couldn't do that with an inspector on her heels.

'Put a call through to the Hôtel Scribe . . . The porter . . .'

A few moments later Maigret was holding the receiver.

'Hello . . . The porter of the Scribe? . . . This is Detective Chief Inspector Maigret . . . How are you, Jean? . . . The children? . . . Fine . . . Perfect . . . I believe you have a regular tenant called Lamotte . . . Victor Lamotte, yes . . . I imagine he rents his apartment by the month? . . . Yes . . . That's what I thought . . .

'Would you put me through to him? . . . I'm sorry? . . . He left yesterday on the Bordeaux express? . . . I thought he didn't usually leave Paris until Saturday evening . . .

'No one asked for him this morning? . . . Did you see a very stout woman, badly dressed, with a bag of groceries in her hand?

'No, I'm not joking . . . Are you sure? . . . Thank you, Jean.'

He knew the porters of all the big hotels in Paris, and there were some that he had seen starting out as bellboys.

Madame Blanc hadn't turned up at the Hôtel Scribe, where she wouldn't, in any case, have found the wine dealer.

'Put me through to his office on Rue Auber.'

He didn't want to miss a chance. On Rue Auber the offices were shut on Saturday, and a clerk who was working late replied. He was on his own in the office. He hadn't seen his boss since two o'clock the previous afternoon.

'Find me the number of Courcel Brothers ball-bearings on Boulevard Voltaire.'

This time, the phone rang in vain in the deserted office. No one there on Saturday, not even a caretaker.

'You should find his address in Rouen. Don't use the word "police". I just want to know if he's at home.'

Fernand Courcel lived in an old town-house on Quai de la Bourse, very close to Pont Boieldieu.

'I'd like to talk to Monsieur Courcel.'

'He's just gone out. This is Madame Courcel speaking.'

The voice was young and playful.

'Can I give him a message?'

'What time do you think he will be back?'

'No later than lunchtime, because we're having friends round.'

'Did he come back this morning?'

'Last night . . . Who's speaking?'

Given Maigret's instructions, Lapointe preferred to hang up.

'He's just gone out. He came back last night. He has to come home to have lunch with friends. His wife has a nice voice.'

'That leaves François Paré. Look for his number in Versailles.'

There too a woman answered, weary and unsympathetic.

'This is Madame Paré.'

'I'd like to talk to your husband.'

'Who is this?'

'A clerk from the ministry,' Lapointe improvised.

'Is it important?'

'Why?'

'Because my husband is in bed. When he came home yesterday he didn't feel well and this morning, after a troubled night, I made him stay in bed. He works too much for a man of his age.'

The inspector felt that she was going to hang up and hurried to ask his question:

'Has he had a visit this morning?'

'What visit?'

'Someone who had a commission for him.'

'No one has been here.'

She hung up without another word.

Florentin and the redhead were at the cemetery when Madame Blanc had disappeared. She hadn't seen any of the three other suspects.

Madame Maigret let him have his lunch in peace, because he seemed preoccupied enough not to add to his worries. It was only when she had poured him his coffee that she asked:

'Have you read the paper?'

'I haven't had time.'

She went to the sitting room and fetched him the morning paper from the coffee table. A big headline first of all:

The crime on Rue Notre-Dame-de-Lorette

Then some more significant sub-headings:

Mysterious meeting Quai des Orfèvres
Detective Inspector Maigret in a fix

He groaned and, before reading the article, went and got a pipe from the rack.

In yesterday's edition we reported in detail on the crime committed in an apartment on Rue Notre-Dame-de-Lorette, the victim of which is a young woman, Joséphine Papet, an unmarried woman without employment.

We suggested that the murderer should be sought among several men who shared the victim's favours.

In spite of the silence observed from the Police Judici-aire, we know that a certain number of individuals were summoned to Quai des Orfèvres yesterday for a general confrontation. It would appear that they included some quite eminent figures.

One of the suspects has attracted more attention than the others, because he was in the apartment when the murder was committed. Did he only witness it? Was he the perpetrator?

Detective Chief Inspector Maigret, who is personally in charge of the investigation, finds himself in a delicate situation. This man, Léon F—, is in fact one of his child-hood friends.

Is this the reason why, in spite of the charges made against him, he is still at liberty? It is hard for us to believe that . . .

Maigret crumpled the newspaper and got to his feet, growling, his teeth gritted:

'The imbeciles!'

Did the indiscretion come from one of the inspectors, who had seen no harm in it and had had it dragged out of him? He didn't know that the reporters were ferreting around all over the place. They must have questioned the concierge, and it wasn't unthinkable that she had proved more talkative than she had with the police.

There had also been the bearded painter, Florentin's neighbour on Boulevard Rochechouart.

'Has that really got to you?'

He shrugged. To tell the truth, the article only added to his perplexity.

Before leaving police headquarters, he had received the ballistic report from Gastinne-Renette, which had confirmed what the forensic doctor had told him. It was a 12-millimetre bullet, a huge calibre, very unusual, and could only have been fired with a Belgian revolver, an old model, impossible to buy commercially.

The expert added that a weapon of that kind was completely inaccurate.

It was obviously the old revolver from the bedside table. Where was it now? There was no point looking for it. It might just as easily have been thrown into the Seine or any sewer, on wasteland, in a field in the countryside.

Why had the murderer taken this compromising object away rather than leaving it where it was? Was he afraid that he might have left prints on it and hadn't had time to get rid of them?

If that was the case, then he also wouldn't have had time to wipe the furniture and objects he had touched.

And yet, in the bedroom, all the prints had been erased, including the ones on the door handles.

Did that lead to the conclusion that the murderer hadn't stayed in the apartment for a quarter of an hour, as Florentin claimed?

And wasn't it Florentin himself who had erased the traces?

All reasoning led back to him. He was the only logical culprit. But Maigret was suspicious of such reasoning.

But he was cross with himself for his patience, which seemed very close to indulgence. Wasn't he allowing himself to be influenced by some kind of childhood loyalty?

'It's completely idiotic,' he said out loud.

'Were you really his friend?'

'Not really . . . In fact, I was irritated by his clowning.'

He didn't add that he sometimes went to the patisserie to see his fellow pupil's sister and blushed.

'I'll see you later.'

She turned her cheek towards him.

'Will you be back for dinner?'

'I hope so.'

It had started raining, and he hadn't noticed. His wife ran down the stairs after him with an umbrella.

On the corner of the boulevard he found an open-platform bus and let himself be rocked back and forth by the movements of the vehicle, vaguely watching those curious animals, human beings, hurrying along the pavements. They were practically running. To go where? To do what?

'If I don't find anything before Monday I'll put him away,' he promised himself, as if to put his conscience at rest.

He walked, under his umbrella, from Châtelet to Quai des Orfèvres. The wind blew in gusts, filled with lashing rain. The water's wet, as he had said when he was a child.

No sooner had he reached his office than there was a knock at the door, and Lourtie came in.

'Bonfils is taking over from me,' he said. 'She came back.'

'At what time?'

'At twelve twenty. I saw her calmly coming down the street holding her bag of groceries.'

'Was it full?'

'At any rate it was fatter and heavier than it was in the morning. She looked at me as she passed in front of me. It seemed as if she was making fun of me. Once she was in her lodge, she took down the sign hanging on the door: "The concierge is on the stairs".'

Maigret paced his office five or six times from window to door and door to window. By the time he came to a standstill he had taken a decision.

'Is Lapointe nearby?'

'Yes.'

'Tell him to wait for me. I'll be right back.'

He took a key from his drawer, the one for the door that communicated between the Police Judiciaire and the Palais de Justice. He walked down the long corridors, climbed a dark staircase and knocked at last on the door of the examining magistrate's office.

Most of the building was silent and deserted. He had little chance of finding Page at work on a Saturday afternoon.

'Come in,' said a voice that seemed far away.

He was there, covered in dust, trying to establish a modicum of order in the little windowless room adjacent to his office.

'You know what, Maigret, I'm finding two-year-old dossiers that have never been classified. It's going to take me months to sort out all the things that my predecessor accumulated in this rag-bag.'

'I've come to ask you for a search warrant.'

'Wait while I wash my hands.'

He had to go to the wash room at the end of the corridor. He was a pleasant and conscientious fellow.

'Have you got any news?'

'The concierge is giving me a hard time. I'm sure that woman knows something. Yesterday, at the confrontation, she was the only one who maintained her composure, and she's probably the only one apart from the party in question who knows who the culprit is.'

'Why would she stay silent? Out of hatred for the police?'

'I don't think that would be enough to make her take risks. I even wondered if the murderer wouldn't try to get rid of her and posted one of my men in front of the house.

'In my view, if she's remaining stubbornly silent, it's because she's been paid to do so. I don't know how much she's been given.

'When she saw how important this case was becoming, she must have thought she hadn't had her full share.

'So this morning, like a skilled professional, she escaped the surveillance of the inspector who was following her. She was careful to go to a butcher's first, to fool him. Once she'd made her purchase, she went just as naturally into a grocery store, and my man wasn't suspicious. It was a quarter of an hour before he noticed that the grocery had a second exit.'

'You don't know where she went?'

'Florentin was with me at Ivry Cemetery. Jean-Luc Bodard came too.'

'Did she see one of the three others?'

'She couldn't have seen any of them. Lamotte went back to Bordeaux yesterday, on the evening express. Courcel is in Rouen and had friends to lunch. As for François Paré, he's sick in bed, and it's his wife's turn to worry.'

'In what name do you want me to issue a warrant?'

'Madame Blanc . . . The concierge.'

The judge looked for a form in the drawer of his desk, filled in the blanks, signed and stamped it.

'I wish you the best of luck.'

'Thank you.'

'By the way, don't worry about the comments in the papers . . . Anyone who knows you . . .'

'Thank you.'

A few minutes later he left Quai des Orfèvres with Lapointe, who was at the wheel. The traffic was dense, the people in more of a hurry than ever, as they were every Saturday. In spite of the rain, in spite of the wind, they were dashing towards the motorways, towards the countryside.

For once, Lapointe immediately found a parking space along the pavement, just outside the house. The lingerie boutique was closed. Only the shoe shop was open, but it was empty, and the shopkeeper, in the doorway, glumly watched the clouds melting into water.

'What are we looking for, chief?'

'Anything that can be of use to us. Probably money . . .'

It was the first time that Maigret had seen Madame Blanc sitting in her lodge. With steel-rimmed spectacles on her round nose, she was reading the afternoon paper, which had just come out.

Maigret pushed the door, followed by Lapointe.

'Have you wiped your feet?'

And, as they didn't reply:

'What do you want from me this time?'

Maigret merely held out the search warrant. She read it and reread it.

'I don't see what that means. What are you going to do?'

'Search the place.'

'Do you mean you're going to go through my things?'

'I'm sorry, believe me.'

'I wonder if I shouldn't call a lawyer.'

'That would prove that you have something to hide. You, Lapointe, keep an eye on her and make sure she doesn't touch anything.'

In a corner of the lodge was a Henri II dresser, whose upper doors were glazed. In that part there were only glasses, a jug and a floral porcelain coffee service.

The drawer on the right contained knives, forks, spoons and a corkscrew as well as three unmatched napkin rings. The cutlery had once been silver-plated, but the brass was now showing through.

The drawer on the left was more interesting, because it contained photographs and papers. One of the photographs showed a couple. Madame Blanc must have been twenty-five and, although she was plump, one couldn't have predicted that she would become the monster she was today. She was even smiling, turned towards a man with a blond moustache who must have been her husband.

In an envelope he found a list of tenants, with the price

of each one's rent. Then, under some postcards, he put his hand on a savings book.

The first payments went back many years. At first they were modest, ten francs, twenty francs a time. Then, regularly, she had set aside fifty francs a month. In January, the month when concierges get tips for the previous year, the sum varied between a hundred and a hundred and fifty francs . . .

In all, eight thousand three hundred and twenty-two francs and a few centimes.

There was no payment from the previous day or the day before that. The last one was a fortnight old.

'You're making progress!'

Undeterred, he went on rummaging. There were plates in the lower part of the dresser, as well as a pile of checked tablecloths.

He lifted the velvet mat that covered the round table in search of a drawer, but the table didn't have one.

On the left was a television set. Nothing but some bits of thread, some drawing pins and a few nails in the drawer of the table that it stood on.

He went into the second room, which wasn't only the kitchen but also served as a bedroom, because there was a bed in an alcove, behind an old curtain.

He started with the bedside table, where he found only a rosary, a missal and a sprig of boxwood. It took him a moment to guess the origin of the sprig of boxwood. It was probably the one that was dipped in holy water when a relation died, and she had kept it as a souvenir.

It was hard to imagine that woman having had a husband. But hadn't she also been a child, like everyone?

He had seen others, men and women, who had been so hardened by life that they had almost been turned into monsters. For years, all her days, all her nights had been spent in these two dark and airless rooms, where she couldn't walk any more than she could have done in a prison cell.

As for the outside world, she knew it only from the visits of the postman and the tenants passing by her window.

In the morning, in spite of her girth and her swollen legs, she had to clean the lift, then the stairs from top to bottom.

And what if she was no longer capable tomorrow?

He felt bad about harassing her and opened a small refrigerator, where he found half a chop, some leftover omelette, two slices of ham and a few vegetables that she had bought that morning.

There was a half-bottle of wine on the table, some clothes and underwear in a cupboard, including a corset and some elasticated knee-pads.

He was ashamed, now, of going on searching, and yet he didn't want to admit defeat. She wasn't a woman who would have settled for promises. If someone had bought her silence, they would have had to pay in cash.

He came back into the lodge and couldn't conceal a flash of anxiety in his eyes.

Then he knew that what he was looking for wasn't in the kitchen. He looked around, slowly. Where had he not searched?

Suddenly, he walked towards the television set. Some magazines were stacked on top of it. One of them showed the daily schedules as well as comments and photographs.

As soon as he opened it, he knew that he had won. The pages were parted where three five-hundred-franc notes and seven hundreds had been slipped inside.

Two thousand two hundred francs. The five-hundred-franc notes were new.

'I assume I'm allowed to save?'

'You forget that I've seen your savings book.'

'So? Am I obliged to put all my eggs in one basket? And what if I need some money all of a sudden?'

'Two thousand two hundred francs all at once?'

'That's my business. I challenge you to cause me trouble over that.'

'You're more intelligent than you look, Madame Blanc. It's as if you'd predicted everything, including today's search. If you'd brought money to the savings bank, the payment would be copied in your book, and I wouldn't have failed to notice the size of the sum and the date . . .

'You don't trust dressers, drawers, unstitched mattresses . . . It's as if you'd read Edgar Allen Poe. You simply slipped the notes into a magazine . . .'

'I haven't stolen from anybody.'

'I'm not claiming you've stolen anything. I'm even convinced that, seeing you behind your door when he was going out, the murderer came to give you that money . . . You still didn't know that a crime had been committed in the building.

'He didn't need to explain why he was so keen that no one should know he had been there that day.

'You know him well, or else he wouldn't be afraid of you.'

'I have nothing to say.'

'When you saw him in my office yesterday afternoon, you sensed that he was very frightened, of you and you alone, because you're the only one who could testify against him.

'Then, this morning, you decided to have another go to get hold of a larger amount, bearing in mind that the freedom of a man, particularly a rich man, is worth more than two thousand two hundred francs.'

As it had the previous day, a vague, a very vague smile, as if smudged by a rubber, floated on her lips.

'You haven't found anyone . . . You've forgotten that it's Saturday.'

The woman still had the same stubborn, enigmatic expression on her round face.

'I'm not saying anything. You can hit me.'

'I don't want to. We will be seeing each other again. Come on, Lapointe.'

And the two men slipped into the little black car.

7.

They did the same as everyone else, in spite of the miserable weather, with only a few sunny spells between one downpour and the next, and went to spend Sunday in the country.

When they had bought the car, they had sworn only to use it to go to their little house in Meung-sur-Loire and during the holidays. They had gone to Meung two or three times, but it was too far only to spend a few hours there, particularly when they found the house empty and Madame Maigret barely had time to dust and prepare a basic meal.

They left at about ten o'clock in the morning.

'Avoiding motorways,' they had agreed.

But thousands of Parisians had had the same idea, and the little roads that should have been so charming were as packed as the Champs-Élysées.

They looked for a nice inn, an enticing menu. Either they were full and they had to wait their turn or the food there was revolting.

But they still started the experiment all over again. It was like the television. When they had bought it, they had promised themselves that they would only watch the most interesting programmes.

After only a fortnight they had changed their seats at the table so that they could face the screen during dinner.

They didn't argue, like most couples, but that didn't mean that Madame Maigret was any less tense at the wheel. With the ink barely dry on her driving licence, she lacked confidence in herself.

'Why don't you overtake?'

'There's a double white line . . .'

That Sunday Maigret barely said a word to her and smoked pipe after pipe, squashed into his seat looking fiercely straight in front of him. In his thoughts, he was on Rue Notre-Dame-de-Lorette, reconstructing every possible scenario of the events that had unfolded in Joséphine Papet's apartment.

The characters became pawns that he moved around the board, trying out every solution. Each of them struck him as plausible for a while, and he attended to every detail, even imagining the dialogue.

Then, when everything seemed to be in place, an objection came into his mind, and everything collapsed.

Then he started again with different pieces. Or else he picked up the same ones and put them in new positions.

They happened upon an inn where the cooking was pretty much as good as what one might have found in a station buffet. The only difference was the size of the bill.

When they tried to go for a little walk in the woods, they found a muddy path, and it started to rain.

They came back early, had cold meat and Russian salad for dinner and then, seeing as Maigret was pacing around the apartment, they went to the cinema.

At nine o'clock on Monday he went into his office. The rain had stopped, the sun was shining, still faintly.

He found the reports of the inspectors who had taken turns keeping Florentin under surveillance.

Florentin had spent Saturday evening in a brasserie on Boulevard de Clichy. It didn't seem to be a place that he normally frequented, and no one said hello to him.

He ordered a beer and sat down beside a table where four regulars who plainly knew each other were playing cards. With his chin propped on an elbow he vaguely followed the game.

At about ten o'clock, one of the players, a thin little man who never stopped talking, announced to the others:

'I'll have to be off, guys. The wife will burn me to a crisp if I'm late, and I'm going fishing tomorrow.'

The others pressed him in vain, and then looked around.

A man with a southern accent asked Florentin:

'Do you play?'

'Yes, sure . . .'

He had taken the seat of the man who had left, and played until midnight while Dieudonné, whose turn it was to keep watch, got bored in his corner.

Good Lord, Florentin had paid for a round with part of the hundred francs that Maigret had given him.

Then he had headed off home and gone to bed after a little complicit wave to the man on his tail.

He had slept in. It was after ten when he reached the café and dunked croissants in his coffee. This time it wasn't Dieudonné but Lagrume who was tailing him, and Florentin looked at him curiously because, to him, Lagrume was a new face.

He was the gloomiest of all the inspectors, afflicted with

a head cold for ten months out of twelve. He also had sensitive flat feet, which made him walk in a curious way.

Florentin had made for a betting shop and filled in his slip, then walked down Boulevard des Batignolles. He hadn't stopped in front of the Hôtel Beauséjour. He probably didn't know that the redhead lived there.

He had eaten lunch in a restaurant on Place des Ternes and then, like two days earlier, he had gone to the cinema.

What would he do with that tall, thin body, his rubber face, when Maigret's hundred francs had run out?

He hadn't met anyone. No one had tried to make contact with him. He had eaten dinner in a self-service restaurant before going home to bed.

The stake-out on Rue Notre-Dame-de-Lorette hadn't produced any more results. Madame Blanc had only left her lodge to put out the bins and give the stairs a sweep.

Some tenants had gone to mass. Others had gone out for the day. The street, almost deserted, was less noisy than on the other days, and the two inspectors who had taken turns to watch it had champed at the bit.

That Monday, Maigret reread all the reports, the one from the pathologist, the one from the armourer and finally the one from Moers and Criminal Records.

A relaxed and refreshed Janvier, full of beans, came into the office after a discreet knock at the door.

'How are you doing, chief?'

'Badly . . .'

'You didn't have a good Sunday?'

'No . . .'

Janvier couldn't help smiling, because he knew that mood and he knew that it was usually a good sign. In the course of an inquiry Maigret soaked everything up like a sponge, people and things, the slightest clues that he recorded unconsciously.

The more he grumbled the heavier he got with everything that he had stored up in this way.

'And what did you do?'

'We went to see my sister-in-law, me, my wife and the kids. There was a fair in the main square, and I don't know how much the children spent shooting at clay pipes.'

Maigret got up and started pacing back and forth. When the bell rang announcing the daily briefing, he muttered:

'They can manage without me.'

He didn't want to answer the questions that the big chief would ask him and was even more reluctant to tell him what he was going to do. Besides, it was still vague. He went on feeling his way.

'If only that appalling creature would talk!'

He was still thinking about that monumental and impassive woman.

'I find myself somehow regretting that we can't use water torture like in olden times. I wonder how much water it would take to fill her up . . .'

He didn't mean it, of course, but it was a way of venting his spleen.

'Have you got any idea?'

Janvier didn't like it when Maigret asked him questions like that and his answer was a little evasive.

'It seems to me . . .'

'It seems to you what? Do you think I've made a colossal blunder?'

'On the contrary. It just seems to me that Florentin knows more about it than she does . . . And Florentin's position is less solid. He has nothing to hope for, except to mope around Montmartre and scrabble a few cents together here and there.'

Maigret looked at him seriously.

'Go and get him.'

He called him back before he disappeared.

'Call in at Rue Notre-Dame-de-Lorette and grab the concierge while you're at it. Let her protest as much as she likes but bring her here by force if necessary.'

Janvier smiled, because he couldn't easily see himself getting to grips with that tower of human flesh that weighed at least twice as much as he did.

A few moments later, Maigret was calling the Ministry of Public Works.

'I'd like to speak to Monsieur Paré, please . . .'

'I'll put you through to his office.'

'Hello! Monsieur Paré?'

'Monsieur Paré isn't here. His wife just called to say he's ill.'

Next, the Versailles number.

'Madame Paré?'

'Who's speaking?'

'Inspector Maigret . . . How is your husband?'

'Not very well. The doctor came and fears it's a nervous collapse.'

'I don't suppose I can speak to him?'

'He's been recommended complete rest.'

'Is he anxious? . . . Has he asked to see the newspapers?'

'No. He's saying nothing. He barely replies with a word or a gesture when I ask him a question.'

'Thank you.'

Then he called the Hôtel Scribe.

'Is that you, Jean? . . . Maigret here . . . Has Monsieur Victor Lamotte come back from Bordeaux? . . . He's already left for his office? . . . Thank you.'

Then the office on Rue Auber.

'I'd like to speak to Monsieur Lamotte . . . This is Inspector Maigret.'

There was a sequence of clicks, as if the call had to pass through a whole hierarchy before reaching the big boss.

'Yes . . .' a dry voice said at last.

'This is Maigret . . .'

'They told me.'

'Do you plan to spend the morning in your office?'

'I don't know.'

'I should ask you not to go out and to wait for me to call you . . .'

'I have to advise you that, if you summon me again, I will be accompanied by my lawyer.'

'That's your right.'

Maigret hung up and called Boulevard Voltaire, where Fernand Courcel had not yet arrived.

'He never gets here before eleven and sometimes he doesn't come on Monday morning. Would you like to talk to the assistant manager?'

'No, thank you.'

As he roamed about his office with his hands behind his back, Maigret had time to run through the hypotheses that he had constructed the previous day when they had gone for a drive.

In the end he had kept only one, with a number of variations. He looked at the clock several times.

Almost ashamed, he opened the cupboard, where he always kept a bottle of brandy. It wasn't there for him, but sometimes he needed it for a client who collapsed at the moment of confession.

He hadn't collapsed. He wasn't the one who was going to have to confess. Nevertheless, he took a long swig straight from the bottle.

He wasn't proud of himself for doing it. He looked impatiently at the clock again. At last he heard the footsteps of several people in the corridor and a furious voice that he recognized: Madame Blanc.

He went and opened the door.

'I'm getting to know this office,' Florentin tried to joke, even though he was worried.

Meanwhile the woman thundered:

'I'm a free citizen, and I demand that . . .'

'Shut her up in an office, Janvier. Stay with her and make sure she doesn't scratch your eyes out.'

And, to Florentin:

'Sit down.'

'I'd rather stand up.'

'And I'd rather see you sitting down.'

'If you insist.'

He pulled a face like in the old days when he had had a row with a teacher and was trying to make the class laugh.

Maigret went and got Lapointe from the neighbouring office. He was the one who had witnessed all the interrogations and who knew the case best.

Maigret took the time to stuff a pipe, light it and tamp down the burning tobacco with a careful thumb.

'I imagine, Florentin, that you still don't have anything to tell me?'

'I've told you what I knew.'

'No.'

'I swear it's the truth.'

'And I'm sure you've been lying all along.'

'Are you calling me a liar?'

'You always were. Even at school.'

'Just for a laugh.'

'Exactly. Well, we aren't laughing here.'

He looked his former classmate in the eyes. He was serious. There was a mixture of contempt and pity on his face. Perhaps more pity than contempt.

'What do you think will happen?'

Florentin shrugged.

'How would I know?'

'You're fifty-three . . .'

'Fifty-four. I was a year older than you, because I resat the first year of secondary.'

'You're getting on a bit, and it won't be easy for you to find another Josée.'

He lowered his head.

'I won't even look for one.'

'Your antiques business is a joke. You have no job, no profession. And these days you don't have the looks to take anyone for a ride.'

It was harsh but necessary.

'You're a mess, Florentin.'

'The whole thing just fell apart . . . I know I'm a failure, but . . .'

'But you go on hoping. Hoping for what?'

'I don't know.'

'Right. Now that we've resolved that question, I'm going to lift a weight from your shoulders.'

Maigret took a moment, looked his old schoolmate in the eyes and said:

'I know you didn't kill Josée.'

8.

The one who was most surprised wasn't Florentin, but Lapointe, who sat there with his pencil in the air and gave his superior a startled look.

'Don't get too excited, because it doesn't mean you're off the hook.'

'But you do admit . . .'

'I admit that there was one point on which you didn't lie, and I still find that surprising of you—'

'I told you—'

'I'd rather you didn't interrupt me. Last Wednesday, at more or less the time you said, probably at about three fifteen, someone rang at the door of the apartment—'

'You see!'

'Will you shut up? As usual, you headed for the bedroom, not knowing who it was. You pricked up your ears, because you and Josée weren't expecting anyone.

'I imagine one of her lovers would occasionally come at a different time from usual, or indeed a different day.'

'In that case, they telephoned.'

'None of them ever came without warning?'

'Very rarely.'

'And in that case you went and hid in the wardrobe. On Wednesday, you weren't in the wardrobe, but in the bedroom. You recognized the voice and you were frightened, because you realized that the visit wasn't for Josée.'

Florentin froze, clearly not understanding how his old schoolmate had reached this conclusion.

'You see, I have proof that someone went upstairs on Wednesday. That someone, frightened by the crime he had just committed, wanted to buy the concierge's silence and gave her everything he had in his pocket: two thousand two hundred francs.'

'You admit that I'm innocent.'

'Of the murder. Although you are indirectly its cause and, if we can talk about morality when it comes to you, you bear the moral responsibility.'

'I don't understand.'

'Yes, you do.'

Maigret got to his feet. He couldn't stay seated for long, and Florentin's eyes followed him around the room.

'Joséphine Papet had a new live-in lover.'

'You mean that redhead?'

'Yes.'

'That was only a passing fancy. He would never have agreed to live with her, to hide, to stay out on certain nights. He's a young fellow, who can get as many girls as he wants.'

'Josée was in love with him, and she'd had enough of you.'

'How do you know? Is that just a supposition on your part?'

'She said so.'

'Who to? Not you, because you never saw her alive.'

'To Jean-Luc Bodard.'

'Do you believe everything that kid tells you?'

'It's not in his interest to lie.'

'What about me?'

'You risk one or two years in prison . . . Probably two, because of your previous convictions.'

Florentin was reacting less and less. He didn't yet know how far Maigret's discoveries would go but he had heard enough to be worried.

'Let's go back to that Wednesday visit . . . Recognizing the voice, you were frightened because, a few days or a few weeks previously, you had started blackmailing one of Josée's lovers.

'Of course, you chose the one you considered the most vulnerable, the one whose respectability was most important to him. You talked to him about his letters.

'How much did you get?'

Florentin lowered his head gloomily.

'Nothing.'

'He wouldn't strike a deal?'

'No, but he asked me for a few days' delay.'

'How much did you ask for?'

'Fifty thousand . . . I wanted it in cash, to get it over with and start a new life somewhere else.'

'So Josée was gradually getting rid of you.'

'It's possible . . . She'd changed . . .'

'You're starting to talk reasonably and, if you continue, I'll help you get out of this without too much damage.'

'You'll do that?'

'You're such an idiot!'

Maigret had said those words very quietly, to himself, but Florentin had heard, and his face had turned crimson.

It was true. There are several thousand people in Paris living on the margins, on more or less obvious swindles, or on the naivety or greed of their fellow men.

They always have some marvellous project that they would only need a few thousand or tens of thousands of francs to turn into reality.

In most cases they end up swindling an idiot and then they have a certain amount of time to live the high life, drive cars and dine in expensive restaurants.

Once the money has gone, they limp along until it starts over again, but barely one in ten of them goes through the courts and experiences prison.

Florentin, on the other hand, had messed up every time, the last time lamentably.

'Now, would you like to talk or do I have to go on?'

'I'd rather you did.'

'The visitor asks to see you. He knows you're in the apartment, because he took the trouble to ask the concierge. He isn't armed. He isn't particularly jealous and he doesn't want anybody to die.

'But he's agitated. Josée, who is worried for you, says you aren't there, she doesn't know where you are.

'He goes into the dining room, walks across it. You hurry towards the bathroom, then, probably, towards the wardrobe.'

'I didn't have time to get there.'

'Fine. He drags you back into the bedroom.'

'Shouting that I'm a good-for-nothing,' Florentin added bitterly. 'And in front of her.'

'She isn't aware of the blackmail. She doesn't understand what's happening. You tell her to be quiet. In spite of everything, you're clinging to those fifty thousand francs that you see as your last chance . . .'

'I can't remember . . . No one knew what he was doing . . . Josée was begging us to calm down . . . The man was furious . . . At some point, because I refused to give him back his letters, he opened the drawer and grabbed the revolver . . .

'Josée started screaming . . . I was scared too and . . .'

'And you went and stood behind her?'

'I swear to you, Maigret, that it was a matter of chance that she took the bullet.

'He clearly wasn't used to holding a gun . . . He was waving his arm about . . . I was about to give him those damned letters when the shot went off . . .

'He looked startled . . . A strange noise came from his throat, and he hurried towards the sitting room . . .'

'Still holding the gun?'

'I suppose so, because I didn't find it again . . . When I bent over Josée, she was dead . . .'

'Why didn't you tell the police?'

'I don't know.'

'I do. You thought about the forty-eight thousand francs that were in the biscuit tin and you wrapped that tin in a newspaper, without thinking that it was that morning's paper.

'As you left, you remembered the letters and stuffed them in your pocket.

'You were going to be rich. Now you had someone to blackmail, not over a liaison, but over a murder . . .'

'What makes you think that?'

'The fact that you wiped the furniture and the door handles. If only your prints alone had been there, they wouldn't have mattered, because you could have denied that you were in the apartment. It was the other man that you were protecting by doing what you did because once he was in prison he wouldn't be worth a fig.'

Maigret sat down heavily again and stuffed a new pipe.

'You went home to put the biscuit tin on top of the wardrobe. At the time you weren't thinking about the letters that were in your pocket. You remembered me and you thought that a former schoolmate wouldn't risk beating you up. You were always afraid of being hit. You remember? There was a little kid, Bambois, if I remember correctly, who scared you just by threatening to pinch your arm.'

'You're cruel.'

'What about you? If you hadn't behaved like a scoundrel, Josée wouldn't be dead.'

'I'll never forgive myself.'

'That won't bring her back to life. And your remorse doesn't concern me. You came to act out your little play and, from the first few words, I knew that something wasn't quite right.

'In the apartment, too, everything seemed fake, twisted, but I couldn't find the thread that would have led me to the truth.

'It was the concierge who intrigued me the most. She's much stronger than you.'

'She could never stand me.'

'And you could never stand her either. By saying nothing about the visitor, she not only earned her two thousand two hundred francs but got you in a terrible mess. As for jumping into the Seine, you made a mistake, because that's what made me think of the letters.

'Obviously you weren't trying to drown yourself. A good swimmer doesn't drown himself by throwing himself off Pont-Neuf, a few metres away from a barge, when the pavements are crammed with people.

'You had just remembered that you had the letters in your pocket. One of my inspectors was on your heels. You could have been searched at any moment.'

'I wouldn't have expected you to guess.'

'I've been in this job for thirty-five years,' Maigret muttered.

He passed into the adjacent office to say a few words to Lucas.

'Don't on any account let them wind you up,' he added.

He came back into his office, where Florentin seemed to have deflated. He was now nothing but a big empty body, a hollow face with evasive eyes.

'If I understand correctly, I'm going to be prosecuted for blackmail?'

'That will depend . . .'

'On what?'

'On the examining magistrate . . . And partly on me too. Don't forget that you wiped the prints so that we wouldn't find the murderer. That could implicate you as an accomplice.'

'You won't do that, will you?'

'I'll talk to the magistrate.'

'A year in prison, two at most, I might be able to bear, but if I have to be locked up for years I'll leave feet first. Even now my heart sometimes shows signs of weakness . . .'

He was bound to ask to be put in the infirmary. This was the boy who had made them laugh in Moulins. When a class had become boring, they turned to him to play the fool.

Because they egged him on. They knew it was what he wanted to do. He would pull new faces, come up with new pranks.

The clown . . . Once he had pretended to drown in the Nièvre, and it took them a quarter of an hour to find him behind some reeds to which he had swum underwater.

'What are we waiting for?' he asked, worried again.

On the one hand, he was relieved to be done with it, while on the other he was worried about seeing his former schoolmate changing his mind.

There was a knock at the door. It was old Joseph, who came and set down a visiting card on Maigret's desk.

'Bring him in. And go and tell Inspector Janvier to bring me the person who is with him.'

He would have given anything for a glass of cold beer, or even another sip of cognac.

'My lawyer, Monsieur Bourdon.'

One of the star figures of the bar, a former president of the association, who had been considered for the Académie Française. Cold and dignified, Victor Lamotte, limping slightly, sat down on one of the chairs and gave Florentin only a distracted glance.

'I assume, inspector, that you have sound reasons for summoning my client? I have learned that on Friday you organized a confrontation whose legality I reserve the right to question.'

'Take a seat, Maître Bourdon,' Maigret replied.

Janvier pushed into the room an agitated Madame Blanc, who immediately froze in front of the lame man.

'Come in, Madame Blanc. Please sit down.'

It looked as if she suddenly found herself faced with a new problem.

'Who's this?' she asked, pointing at Maître Bourdon.

'Your friend Monsieur Lamotte's lawyer.'

'Have you arrested him?'

Her eyes were bulging more than ever.

'Not yet, but I will in a few moments. You acknowledge, do you not, that it was he who, last Wednesday, on his way down from Mademoiselle Papet's apartment, gave you two thousand two hundred francs to keep quiet?'

She gritted her teeth without replying.

'You were wrong to give her that money, Monsieur Lamotte. The size of the sum gave her a taste for it. She thought if her silence had been bought at that price, it must be worth even more.'

'I don't know what you're talking about.'

The lawyer frowned.

'Let me explain why it was you that I ended up choosing among several suspects. On Saturday, Madame Blanc, whom I had left under the surveillance of an inspector, managed to lose him by going into a shop with two exits. She wanted to see you to demand an extra payment. And she was in a hurry, because she was afraid that I would arrest you at any moment.'

'I didn't see that woman on Saturday.'

'I know. What matters is that she looked for you. Three of you each had your day: François Paré on Wednesday, Courcel from Thursday evening until Friday . . . Jean-Luc Bodard was more irregular.

'Generally speaking a provincial tradesman who comes and spends a few days on business in Paris every week goes home on Saturday. And yet that wasn't true in your case, because your Saturday afternoon was devoted to Mademoiselle Papet.

'The concierge knew it, and that's why she tried to see you. She didn't know that since you no longer had an appointment you had left Paris the previous day.'

'Ingenious,' the lawyer said, 'but I doubt that a jury will be satisfied with such slender evidence.'

The concierge said nothing, heavier and more motionless than ever.

'Of course, I won't arrest your client on that basis. Léon Florentin here has confessed everything.'

'I thought he was the alleged culprit.'

Florentin, shoulders hunched, no longer dared to look at anyone.

'Not the culprit,' Maigret replied. 'The victim.'

'I don't follow you.'

Victor Lamotte had followed him and shifted on his chair.

'He was the one at whom, in theory, the gun was being pointed. He was the one that Monsieur Lamotte threatened, in order to get hold of some compromising letters. As it happens, he is a very bad marksman, and the gun wasn't very accurate either.'

'Is that true?' the lawyer asked his client.

He hadn't expected the discussion to take such a turn. Lamotte didn't reply and glared fiercely at Florentin.

'I should add, for the sake of your argument, that I am not sure your client killed deliberately. He is a man who doesn't like opposition, and being contradicted puts him in a rage. Unfortunately, he had a gun in his hand, and the shot went off . . .'

This time Lamotte trembled and turned towards Maigret in astonishment.

'If you would wait for me for a moment.'

Maigret repeated the journey along the corridors of the Palais that he had made on Saturday. He knocked at the door of the examining magistrate and found him immersed in a thick folder, while the clerk had taken over the tidying of the back room.

'Finished!' Maigret announced, slumping on a chair.

'He confessed?'

'Who?'

'Well . . . that fellow Florentin, I assume . . .'

'He didn't kill anybody. But I need an arrest warrant in his name. Grounds: attempted blackmail . . .'

'And the murderer?'

'He's waiting in my office with his lawyer, Maître Bourdon.'

'That will give us a headache. He's one of the most—'

'He will be very compliant. I won't go so far as to say that it was an accident, but there are many extenuating circumstances.'

'Which of the two . . .'

'The lame one, Victor Lamotte, a wine dealer from Chartrons, Bordeaux, where matters of dignity, precedence and, incidentally, morality are not taken lightly.

'This afternoon I will draw up my report, and I hope to be able to give it to you before the end of the day. It's almost lunchtime and . . .'

'You're hungry?'

'Thirsty!' Maigret admitted.

A few minutes later, in his office, he was handing the documents signed by the magistrate to Lapointe and Janvier.

'Take them to Criminal Records to get the formalities out of the way and then drop them off at the cells.'

Janvier asked, pointing at the concierge who had risen to her feet:

'What about her?'

'We'll see about that later. In the meantime, let her go home. The lodge can't be left empty for ever.'

She looked at him, her eyes blank. Her lips began to move, like water bubbling on a stove, but she said nothing and made for the door.

'Will you join me at the Brasserie Dauphine, boys?'

It was only afterwards that it occurred to him that it might have been cruel to mention this arrangement with his colleagues out loud in front of two men who were going to be locked up.

Five minutes later, at the bar of the familiar little restaurant, part of which was a bistro, he said:

'A beer. In the biggest glass you have.'

In thirty-five years, he hadn't met a single one of his
fellow pupils from the Lycée Banville.

And of all people it had to be Florentin!

OTHER TITLES IN THE SERIES

MAIGRET'S PATIENCE
GEORGES SIMENON

'Maigret felt less light at heart than when he had woken up that morning with sunlight streaming into his apartment or when he had stood on the bus platform, soaking up images of Paris coloured like in a children's album. People were often very keen to ask him about his methods. Some even thought they could analyse them, and he would look at them with mocking curiosity.'

When a gangster Maigret has been investigating for years is found dead in his apartment, the Inspector continues to bide his time and explore every angle until he finally reaches the truth.

Translated by David Watson

OTHER TITLES IN THE SERIES

MAIGRET AND THE NAHOUR CASE
GEORGES SIMENON

'Maigret had often been called on to deal with individuals of this sort, who were equally at home in London, New York and Rome, who took planes the way other people took the Metro, who stayed in grand hotels . . . he had trouble suppressing feelings of irritation that might have been taken for jealousy.'

A professional gambler has been shot dead in his elegant Parisian home, and his enigmatic wife seems the most likely culprit – but Inspector Maigret suspects this notorious case is far more complicated than it appears.

Translated by Will Hobson

OTHER TITLES IN THE SERIES

MAIGRET'S PICKPOCKET
GEORGES SIMENON

'Maigret would have found it difficult to formulate an opinion of him. Intelligent, yes, certainly, and highly so, as far as one could tell from what lay beneath some of his utterances. Yet alongside that, there was a naïve, rather childish side to him.'

Maigret is savouring a beautiful spring morning in Paris when an aspiring film-maker draws his attention to a much less inspiring scene, one where ever changing loyalties can have tragic consequences.

Translated by Sian Reynolds

OTHER TITLES IN THE SERIES

MAIGRET HESITATES
GEORGES SIMENON

'Maigret looked at him in some confusion, wondering if he was dealing with a skilful actor or, on the contrary, with a sickly little man who found consolation in a subtle sense of humour.'

A series of anonymous letters lead Maigret into the wealthy household of an eminent lawyer and a curious game of cat and mouse with Paris high society.

Translated by Howard Curtis

OTHER TITLES IN THE SERIES

MAIGRET IN VICHY
GEORGES SIMENON

'What else did they have to do with their days? They ambled around casually. From time to time, they paused, not because they were out of breath, but to admire a tree, a house, the play of light and shadow, or a face.'

While taking a much-needed rest cure in Vichy with his wife, Maigret feels compelled to help with a local investigation, unravelling the secrets of the spa town's elegant inhabitants.

Translated by Ros Schwartz

OTHER TITLES IN THE SERIES